Praise for *Chrissy's Cozy Mystery Series*

Diane Wing continues Chrissy and Autumn's love story with a little murder mystery hijinks thrown in! Once again I am left wondering till the end who the murderer is. Mrs. Wing throws some new and interesting characters into the storyline of *A Winter's Tail*, and they fit in seamlessly with the current cast of old friends. I love how the animals, Chrissy, Ace along with Mickey and others, don't just play second fiddle to the human characters. Each canine has their own identity and a necessary part of the plot. Kudos to Mrs. Wing for another great cozy afternoon read!

—Antoinette Brickhaus, Leonardtown, MD

The fourth installment of the Chrissy the Shih Tzu cozy mysteries finds Chrissy's pet parent, Autumn, preparing for her wedding to Ray Reed, a local police lieutenant. Autumn's friend and cousin, Bea, is worried that Autumn and Ray's nuptials are cursed because of several setbacks to Autumn's plans. Meanwhile, Chrissy discovers a body in a snow pile and Ray is assigned to investigate the victim's death. This is the best book of the series so far! I couldn't figure out who was sabotaging Autumn and Ray's wedding, who killed the local psychotherapist, and how the events were related. A fun, cute, and enjoyable read.

—Terri Chalmers, Sicklerville, NJ

What a fun read! Treat yourself to *A Winter's Tail*—the gripping addition to Diane Wing's wildly popular Chrissy's Mysteries cozy. You are invited to join the festivities and celebrate the wedding of the year! Autumn Clarke will marry the love of her life, Ray Reed, at a spectacular holiday event at the newly renovated Peabody Mansion... until Chrissy, the amazing Shih Tzu sleuth, discovers a fresh corpse in a downtown snowdrift during a festive wedding-planning shopping spree. Things turn dark and strange as Autumn encounters a series of bizarre and shocking events before their wedding day. Is it truly a cursed event, or is it a vengeful foe returning for the ultimate revenge and desecration of Autumn and Ray's happily ever after? Snuggle in for this delightful treat!

—Maxine Ashcraft, Oakland, CA

Autumn and Chrissy are turning me into a cozy mystery fan. Chrissy once again discovers all-important clues to help solve the murder mystery. In this installment the glamour of Hollywood comes East along with an unsolved murder. How this impacts the big Halloween party creates a great opportunity to develop an exciting plot.

—Steven Cohen

This series has a calming effect on me. The author does a wonderful job of writing a page turning mystery that you can get lost in for hours. Even though it is a work of fiction, when you put the book down you feel renewed and refreshed. There is a lot of character development in this series and I enjoy seeing how the characters have developed throughout the three books. I am looking forward to seeing where the author takes the series next!

Marie McNary, *A Cozy Experience*

I loved getting to know the characters better, their interactions and the motives that drive them. The dogs however need a special mention from the stoic guardian Ace to the adorable, clue sniffing Chrissy and their utter commitment to the humans that they have taken under their paw.

—Krystyna's Reviews

Through the relationship between Autumn and Chrissy, Wing also shows the importance of therapy animals and how much they can help those who need them. Add a sweet romance to the intrigue of the mystery and you've got a book that you won't want to put down.

—Melissa Alvarez, Intuitive, animal communicator and author of *Animal Frequency and Llewellyn's Little Book of Spirit Animals*

Diane Wing has created a wonderfully endearing little character in Chrissy the Shih Tzu. It really shines through that the author is a lover of animals and dogs. I can see these books quickly becoming a cherished addition to the cozy mystery genre.

—J. New, author of *The Yellow Cottage Vintage Mysteries*

Any book worth remembering has lessons under the surface. I approve of Chrissy's Mysteries. They are mostly about human nature, and the way good people treat each other. Read, and find out what I mean.

—Bob Rich, PhD, author of *Sleeper, Awake!*

A Winter's Tail

A Chrissy the Shih Tzu
Cozy Mystery

Diane Wing

Modern History Press

Ann Arbor, MI

ISBN 978-1-61599-622-3 paperback
ISBN 978-1-61599-623-0 hardcover
ISBN 978-1-61599-624-7 eBook

Published by
Modern History Press   www.ModernHistoryPress.com
5145 Pontiac Trail   info@ModernHistoryPress.com
Ann Arbor, MI   tollfree 888-761-6268
                              fax 734-663-6861

Distributed by Ingram (USA/CAN/AU), Bertram's Books (UK/EU)
Audiobook editions available at Audible.com and iTunes

For the fur babies who enrich our lives

Books by Diane Wing....

Cozy Mysteries with Chrissy the Shih Tzu

Attorney-at-Paw

The Dog-Eared Diary

Trick-or-Doggy Treat

A Winter's Tail

Dark Fantasy

Coven: The Scrolls of the Four Winds

Thorne Manor and other bizarre tales

Trips to the Edge

Non-fiction

The True Nature of Tarot: Your Path to Personal
Empowerment, 10th Anniversary Ed.

The True Nature of Energy: Transforming Anxiety into
Tranquility

The Happiness Perspective: Seeing Your Life Differently

Acknowledgements

I'm grateful to all the people who contributed to the creation of this book. The food maven, Chef Jacqueline Peccina Kelly, created the wedding menu and provided scrumptious recipes at the end of this book. Thanks to the beta readers, without whom I'd stay in my own head: Maxine Ashcraft, Antoinette Brickhaus, and Terri "Eagle Eye" Chalmers. Special thanks to Judge Patricia Richmond for her guidance on legal ethical questions. Much gratitude to Sergeant Roger Gillispie of the Abington Police Department for giving me insight into police procedure and guidelines. I appreciate the feedback of Bob Rich, Ph.D. for doing the final edits and catching issues no one else saw. And last but never least, many thanks to my publisher, Victor Volkman, for his support, guidance, and trust. I'm so fortunate to have all of these wonderful people in my circle.

Notes

Book club questions, recipes of meals from the book, appear at the end of the book. Enjoy!

This work was professionally edited and proofread. However, if you encounter any typos or formatting issues, please contact info@ModernHistoryPress.com so we can correct it.

Dramatis Personae

Brittany Farmer—Owner of Tying the Knot, a wedding accessories shop

Megan Harris—Owner of the bridal shop, With This Ring

Pamela Brown—Scandal/gossip podcaster

William Moore—Detective in New Hope

Terri Cromwell—local judge who lives in New Hope

Harry Halifax—Award-winning ice sculptor

Faith Halifax—Harry's wife

Angela Curry—Victim and therapist who knows people's secrets

Barry Cromwell—Terri Cromwell's son

Dr. Tim O'Brien—Psychiatrist at the hospital

Chief Bruce Stanley—New Hope police chief

Officer Jim Osgood—New Hope police officer

Frank Pangborn—Limousine driver and private detective

Mayor Josh Snyder—Knollwood Mayor

Carol Reed—Ray's mom

Kevin Reed—Ray's dad

Jodi Fallston—Professional Executor/Attorney for Angela Curry

Ward Everly—Landscaper for the Peabody Mansion B&B and protector of the family

Elizabeth Johnson—event planner and décor designer

Autumn Clarke—Chrissy's mommy and owner of the Peabody Mansion B&B

Kim Stokes—Assistant manager, Peabody Mansion B&B

Stella Clarke—Autumn's Mother

Sarah Kelly—Chef for the Inn

George Clarke—Autumn's Father

Chrissy—Autumn's Dog and pet detective

Stephanie Douglas—Autumn's Best Friend & 5th grade teacher

Steve Coleman—Neighbor, Father of Lisa Coleman, and Mickey's pet parent

Lisa Coleman—Steve's daughter and owner of Coleman's Kitchen

Mickey—Standard poodle and Chrissy's best friend

Raymond Reed—Lieutenant in Knollwood Police Department, Groom, and pet parent to Ace

Ace—Ray Reed's German shepherd dog

Maureen Roberts—Realtor

Beatrice Peabody—Autumn's cousin

Brad Hall—Neighbor, Julie's husband, and pet parent to Teddy the Yorkshire terrier

Julie Hall—Neighbor, Brad Hall's wife, and pet parent to Teddy the Yorkshire terrier

Teddy—Chrissy's Yorkshire terrier friend

Dr. Wesley Harper—Autumn's psychiatrist

Stacey Eldridge—bookshop owner, town historian, knows about wedding superstitions

Clay—Stacey's miniature poodle

Adam Miller—Knollwood Police officer, Stephanie's boyfriend, and Ray's best man

Obituary: Angela Curry, Ph.D. (1980-2021), New Hope, PA

Psychologist Angela Curry, 41, died December 1, 2021. She was born in New Hope and attended school in Philadelphia, where she earned her Ph.D. in Clinical Psychology from Drexel University. Dr. Curry returned to New Hope and opened her private practice.

Dr. Curry published articles on the treatment of post-traumatic stress disorder, schizophrenia, and anxiety disorders in the *Annual Review of Clinical Psychology* and *Clinical Psychology Review.*

She was the last member of the Curry family.

In her final wishes, she asked for donations to the National Alliance on Mental Illness in her name.

It was the worst November they could remember, and so early in the season. Most years the snow waited until Thanksgiving to make its first appearance with flurries. But this year, back-to-back snowstorms hit Bucks County, and everyone was tired of shoveling and the sound of snow blowers. Roadside snow piles grew higher with each storm. Days above thirty-five degrees were few, but when they came, they did little to thaw the deep snow piles, as the cold, dense air sank to ground level and maintained the frozen drifts.

Autumn did what she could to make it more bearable for Chrissy, her precious Shih Tzu, but the 16-pound ball of fur with short little legs struggled in the snow. Even her pink suede and Sherpa fleece-lined winter coat with matching snow boots that stayed on for a minute-and-a-half at most didn't make trudging in the snow to do her business any easier. Autumn dug out a space in the yard that led from the patio to a large, open circle for Chrissy to mark.

Today, Autumn had to drive to New Hope to address some wedding details, like picking up the invitations that were already late. The wedding was in two weeks. Good thing she'd sent an email a couple of weeks ago to hold the date for December 11th, but the major obstacle to holding the wedding on that date was the weather. She had no intention of putting her guests at risk, especially since she owned the venue and could change the date whenever she chose. The Peabody Mansion Bed & Breakfast was hers and available any time, since she decided to not officially open until January.

She and Chrissy parked in the fully plowed municipal parking area in town. Autumn lifted Chrissy from her car seat and clicked the pink-with-rhinestones leash onto the metal loop of the harness that poked through the opening of her pink snow jacket. To get to the shoveled sidewalk, she held Chrissy while she navigated the narrow paths from the parking lot to the main walkway and placed her treasured cargo onto the sidewalk.

Chrissy shook beneath the thick jacket and waited for her mommy to walk, staying by her side. Autumn noticed the large chunks of snowmelt pellets on the sidewalk and hoped it was the paw-friendly type. She had baby wipes in her purse to use on Chrissy's paws once they got to their destination.

The bell tinkled a welcome into the charming wedding shop that provided brides with invitations, party favors, cards, champagne flutes, hair accessories, and wedding décor. The brisk walk from the parking lot made Autumn appreciate the warmth surrounding her when she closed the door. She wiped her feet on the doormat and crouched down to clean Chrissy's paws.

"Weather's not fit for man nor beast," said Brittany Farmer from behind the open-front, ornate cream-colored desk and matching carved chair. She wore her shiny black hair long and straight. Her elaborate makeup included smoky eyes and bright red lipstick. Long, red nails and lots of rings accentuated the tight black jumpsuit that clung to her curvy figure.

"Hi Brittany," said Autumn. "You're certainly right about the weather."

"Risky, having a December wedding," Brittany commented.

"We didn't want to wait until spring. I'm sure everything will be fine."

Chrissy went under the desk to sniff Brittany's black spike-heeled shoes, shook her head when Brittany tried to pet her, and then went over to the wall and explored the wedding favors with her nose.

"Come here, sweetheart." Autumn gently tugged her leash.

"She's fine," said Brittany, rising from her chair. "I'll be right back with your invitations. I know they're late, but I have no control over the printer's schedule."

She sashayed to the back room.

Autumn looked around the store to see if she was forgetting anything. She still hadn't decided whether to wear a veil or a headband with crystals. She'd bring her cousin Beatrice to the bridal shop with her to see what looked best with the antique gown. After all, Bea was the one who'd found the dress in the attic and suggested Autumn wear it. Bea was an unknown cousin found when Autumn had inherited the Peabody fortune. As rough going as it was in the beginning, they grew close and now were a part of each other's lives.

Brittany returned with a cardboard box and placed it on the desk. Autumn opened the box and saw a different font than she had chosen, inviting people to join her on December 27th to witness her marriage to Raymond Rudd. Not only were they late, the invitations were completely wrong.

She looked at Brittany, astounded.

"Did you check these when they came in?"

"No, the printer is superb, so there's no need."

"These invitations not only give the wrong information, but aren't in the font I chose."

Brittany glanced at them and said, "Oh. Well, I guess it's getting late in the game to have them redone."

Brittany owned the shop, and Autumn, shocked by her nonchalant attitude toward the botched order, held back her anger. Chrissy head-butted Autumn's leg and took her out of the headspace that could result in an outburst. Chrissy was astute at reading Autumn's moods and how to get her back to center. Autumn picked up her smart little girl, feeling the intensity subside.

She felt her feet on the floor and then said, "Well, I'm not paying for these."

Brittany shrugged. "It's the printer's fault, so he'll have to eat it."

Autumn preferred to support local businesses, and even with her hopes of getting wedding referrals for the bed-and-breakfast, there was no way she would recommend Brittany or do business with her from now on.

Without a word, Autumn and Chrissy left the shop. The frigid air hit their faces and cooled down Autumn's emotional heat. She kissed Chrissy on the head and put her down. Chrissy shook and looked up at Autumn.

"Let's take a little walk and get rid of some of this negative energy," she said to Chrissy, who followed Autumn's lead. Chrissy pranced down the sidewalk like nothing major had just happened. Autumn watched her and went into an in-the-moment perspective, where Brittany didn't exist and her wedding invitations weren't a disaster. This little fluff ball had taught Autumn so much about being centered and joyful.

They walked past piles of dirty snow that lined the streets. Chrissy occasionally sniffed the piles and then moved on. They walked down Main Street and looked in the windows of a boutique, a jewelry shop, and a bookstore. Autumn went into the bookstore and bought the latest mystery fiction from one of her favorite authors. She had so many unexplored volumes at the Peabody mansion, but most were antique. She wanted some current books to read, even as she went through the older volumes. They walked past side streets, where charming townhouses and small single-family dwellings stood tightly packed.

With all the snow, the township prohibited parking on the street. The barrier of snow between the sidewalk and the street blocked them from crossing, except where paths opened to access the crosswalk. The snow was especially free of street grime in a pile just before the crosswalk ahead. As they came closer, Chrissy put her nose to the sidewalk and followed it to the pile. Her sniffing intensified until her face pushed into the snow. She wagged her tail and looked at Autumn before digging.

"What did you find?" Autumn asked.

Chrissy's digging accelerated, her paws digging deeper. Autumn tried pulling her away, but she resisted. Bright red dots showed through the indentation before a gloved hand appeared. That's when Autumn picked up Chrissy, who reluctantly relinquished her quest, and hit Ray Reed's number on speed dial. Autumn's fiancé, Ray, and his loyal German shepherd dog, Ace, a retired police dog, would bring the troops to manage the situation.

~ 2 ~

As a lieutenant with the Knollwood police department, Ray's relationship with the New Hope chief of police, Bruce Stanley, was collaborative and friendly. Each municipality ran on a tight budget and a lean staff, so they partnered when needed.

Within a half hour of Autumn's urgent call, police were on site and the area cordoned off with yellow tape. A crowd had gathered near the area and cars driving by rubbernecked to see what was going on.

Ray stood on the sidewalk with Ace, who guarded Chrissy and Autumn. He looked down at Chrissy.

"What is it with you, little one? Is it your destiny to uncover dead bodies?"

Chrissy smiled her doggy smile and licked her nose, which was running from the cold.

"I hope not," Autumn answered for Chrissy. "This better be the last one."

"Maybe we should swear her in as a detective," said Ray.

Autumn playfully punched his arm.

The moment of joking quickly passed as they focused their attention on the body being dug out from the ice-encrusted snow pile. A deep wound in the center of the chest made Autumn cringe.

Ray inspected the body. A V-shaped puncture differed from knife and gunshot wounds he'd witnessed in his years on the police force or even as a soldier in Afghanistan.

Autumn asked, "Do you recognize her?"

"No, but it looks like her purse is with the body. We'll find out soon enough."

Autumn rubbed her arms and noticed Chrissy shivering. She opened her coat, picked up Chrissy, and snuggled her inside, closing the coat so Chrissy's head stuck out.

"You two are freezing," said Ray. "Go home, and we'll come over after we're finished here."

"Okay. I'll take Ace with us, too."

"Good." Ray squeezed Autumn's gloved hand.

Autumn gave a tired smile and nodded.

❅ ❅ ❅

Chrissy came in from playing her new game of what Autumn called *snow pile*. Chrissy liked to take a running leap, land in the snow up to her chest, and then push her face into the dense whiteness. Snow clumped above her eyes, around her nose, and under her chin. Chrissy's doggy smile looked like a clown face amidst the dangling chunks of snow and made Autumn laugh. A good shake freed only some of it and left compact balls of snow clinging to Chrissy's luxurious locks.

Ace watched instead of playing the game, but his fur also had balls of snow clinging to his underbelly.

Both seemed unfazed after this morning's discovery of a dead woman hidden in a snow pile on a public street. Autumn, however, was tense from the encounter over the wedding invitations, followed by Chrissy the detective finding another body. She called Beatrice to come hang out by the fire to talk it through.

Autumn loved the cozy way snow made her feel inside her childhood home and loved sharing it. The blazing fire in the stone fireplace crackled and helped to melt the winter chill from Chrissy, Ace, and Beatrice. Chrissy's pink and white striped bath towel and a larger sage green towel for Ace warmed on the hearth. Bea had a warm cloth to work on the snow clinging to Ace's fur as he lay on his side, while Autumn held Chrissy in her lap, gently removing caked snow from her face and paws.

Autumn grabbed the soft towel from the hearth and dried Chrissy, then finished the process with a kiss to the top of her head and a little squeeze before putting her down on the floor. Chrissy shook and charged across the den, wiggled under her dog bed, which was piled with toys, and, tail wagging, lifted her body, scattering them all over the floor. She looked over at them, tongue flopping from an endearing, mischievous grin. Autumn and Bea laughed.

Bea finished drying Ace, and he ran over to where Chrissy batted a ball across the floor toward her mommy. Autumn picked it up and tossed it across the room, Chrissy in hot pursuit. Ace stopped the ball from going under a chair and waited for Chrissy to catch up.

"I've been talking to Stacey," said Bea.

Stacey Eldridge owned the local bookstore and oversaw the historical wing of the Peabody Mansion Museum. As the town historian, her knowledge extended beyond local lore and into surprising subjects. Her miniature poodle, Clay, was a friend of Chrissy's.

"She told me about wedding superstitions and all the things that could go wrong if they're not heeded. A curse could befall the ceremony or your marriage. I'm trying to avoid a wedding disaster."

"We've already had one with the invitations," Autumn answered. A flash of her ruined invitations popped into her mind. "Even so, I don't believe in curses."

"See, it's already happening. I should go down to that shop and give Brittany a piece of my mind!" Beatrice groused.

Autumn considered letting her. Bea could be quite intimidating, as she'd learned early in their relationship. After a small, internal debate, Autumn decided against it. She wanted to put the incident behind her and move on.

"The operative word is superstition. I can order new invitations online, and they might be even better than the original ones would have been. Think of all the things that can go right. Everyone associated with the wedding wants the best for us, and that brings luck."

"Wouldn't luck be a superstition?"

Autumn paused. "Okay. I concede that the idea of luck is also superstitious. So, if I knock on wood," she stood and rapped her knuckles against the mahogany mantle, "then we should be okay." Autumn laughed at her own joke.

Bea smiled. "Ah, so you do believe," she said, crossing her arms in triumph. "All I'm saying is that a Wednesday would be better than Saturday. Stacey said Saturday is the unluckiest day to get married. Followed by Thursday, according to English. Maybe it's divine intervention. When you reorder the invitations, just change the date to the eighth or the fifteenth."

"All I know is that I'm lucky to be marrying Ray, and love brings everything good, so any day will do, but Saturday is when the most people can attend."

Chrissy and Ace galloped past, each with a squeaky toy in their mouth. The sound increased their excitement, making them chew harder to make even more ruckus. Autumn pictured them having so much fun together when Ray and Ace moved in.

"How many people did you invite?"

"About one hundred. We'll have it at the Peabody Mansion. Ten tables in the living room, buffet set up in the lobby. Plenty of room for milling about."

Chrissy had swapped her toy for a ball and brought it over to Autumn, dropping it in front of her, tail wagging furiously. Autumn bounced the ball, and Chrissy hopped after it, pinning it into the corner, where she growled playfully. That was Autumn's signal to come over and try to take the ball away from her. She crawled across the floor toward her fur baby, who saw her, and went for the ball more aggressively, protecting it from Autumn. Reaching around Chrissy, she pretended to try to take it away, finally grasping the now soaked ball and tossing it across the room. Chrissy ran after it but tired of the game, and trotted over to where Autumn knelt on the floor. Autumn lifted her fur baby and settled onto the deep-cushioned chair next to the fireplace so Chrissy could snuggle on her mommy's lap. Ace opted for his spot in front of the fire.

"What about the ceremony?"

"There's a beautiful spot down the trail next to the old sycamore tree. My arborist said it's likely 200 years old."

"I love that tree," agreed Bea. "Even without leaves it's so majestic."

"It's a symbol of love, support, protection, and fertility," said Autumn, rubbing Chrissy's soft body. "It's also the tree of gifts. It's perfect to have a wedding ceremony there."

"Maybe in the spring, but it's a bit chilly for an outdoor wedding."

"Elizabeth said we could get outdoor heat lamps to surround the area, the kind restaurants use."

Elizabeth Johnson was the Peabody Mansion decorating and event planning consultant. She did a marvelous job organizing the Halloween event. Her creativity gave rise to a festive and spooky atmosphere. Autumn looked forward to seeing what she planned for the wedding's winter theme.

Autumn stroked Chrissy's silky hair. "And you, my little lovey, are going to be my flower girl."

Chrissy sleepily grunted in agreement.

The doorbell rang, and Chrissy sprung off the chair and ran barking toward the door, with Ace close behind. The tone of her barks let Autumn know who was at the door. She had a high-pitched bark when it was Ray and Ace, but this bark had a slightly lower tone, a signal that Mickey, the standard poodle, and his human, Autumn's neighbor, Steve Coleman, were at the door.

"Hey guys!" Autumn welcomed them in. She grabbed the towel she kept by the door for wet paws and bent to dry Mickey's large, well-groomed paw. "Come on in."

Steve unhooked Mickey's leash from his collar. The poodle, Ace, and Chrissy exchanged sniffs and then trotted to the kitchen to wait for a snack in front of the cabinet they knew held goodies. Autumn kept several types of treats for the pups and went through the ritual of letting them smell each one before choosing the one they wanted. When Chrissy decided on her snack, Mickey usually followed suit and ate the same one. Ace decided independently of the other two.

"So spoiled," said Steve, watching the scene play out as he had many times before.

"That's their job," said Bea from behind them. Not having been a dog-lover in the past, connecting with Autumn and seeing the love she and Chrissy shared lifted her heart. It helped her understand unconditional love and made her consider getting a dog of her own someday.

A couple rounds of snacks and a good long drink of filtered water later, the pups satiated, they galloped into the den. Steve peeked around the wall and saw them each pick a toy—Mickey, a large rope, Ace, a long, stuffed toy with multiple squeakers, and Chrissy a small stuffed pig—and settle in for a chewing session.

If only that was all it took to feel content in life. Steve's health problems weighed on him most days. Watching the canine friends made him vow to make the most of each day and enjoy the moment.

"How about some hot chocolate?" Autumn asked, putting the ingredients onto the granite counter next to the stove.

Grabbing a silver pot from the island cabinet, she remembered her mother saying it was the perfect size to make hot chocolate for three people. Back then, it had meant Autumn, her father, George Clarke, and her mother, Stella Clarke; a cherished memory she held onto.

When her parents had died in a car accident with Autumn in the back seat, the devastation was overwhelming. The trauma of the accident and losing her parents resulted in post-traumatic stress disorder. Therapy for the condition included adopting Chrissy, who helped Autumn heal, while she did the same for Chrissy, traumatized by the loss of her pet parent. Autumn was no longer alone in the world. She had Chrissy, Ray, wonderful friends and neighbors, and now Beatrice.

Autumn topped the steaming, rich chocolate with mini marshmallows and handed Bea and Steve an oversized mug printed with snowflakes and friendly snowmen.

"I'm thinking of having a hot chocolate bar at the wedding," she said, cradling her mug as she led the others into the den.

Bea blew on her drink and took a tentative sip. The marshmallows were just starting to melt, making the chocolate even creamier. "Great idea! That's where you'll find me if you need me at the wedding."

Autumn watched Chrissy attack her pink piggy and pull at the toy's tummy. She was on the verge of ripping the seam apart again. That's why Autumn bought this same toy five at a time, so her baby had a back-up.

"Did you hear about the body they found in a snowdrift?" Steve asked. He sipped his beverage. He had a way of delivering horrific news as though he was talking about clipping coupons.

"Of course," Bea replied, pointing a thumb toward Autumn. "I'm tired of reports of dead bodies in the area."

"Yes, Chrissy actually found her," said Autumn. "Did they identify the body?"

Steve paused for dramatic effect. "Angela Curry, Ph.D. She's a psychotherapist in New Hope. Her office is across the street from where they found her body."

Autumn thought for a moment. She had been so focused on window shopping that she hadn't noticed an office.

"How did you find out? Ray hasn't called yet to let me know," she asked.

"Pamela Brown's podcast. I listen every day on my phone," said Steve.

"The gossip columnist?" asked Bea, as Ace came over and dropped his moist rope toy at her feet.

"He likes you," said Autumn.

"Great," said Bea, picking up the rope toy with her thumb and forefinger and tossing it far enough so that Ace could run after it. She rubbed her fingers vigorously with her napkin to get the slime off of them.

Steve asked, "Are you thinking of getting a dog of your own, Bea? "It'd be nice to add another furry friend to this circle."

Mickey ran over to his daddy and plunked down at his feet. Steve rubbed his fluffy head, a perfect poodle topknot.

"I'm thinking about it, but not completely convinced just yet."

"Back to Pamela," said Autumn. "The police have barely processed the body. How could she know?"

"On her show, she talks about her knack for being in the right place at the right time," Steve said.

"Or she has someone on the inside feeding her information," Autumn thought out loud.

3

Ray walked in the door as Autumn prepared dinner. He kissed Autumn and saw that Chrissy and Ace were already eating theirs. They looked up, gave him a brief wag, and put their heads back into their bowls.

Autumn saw the disappointed look on Ray's face.

"You know they focus on their food and then give you a welcome home," Autumn assured him.

He nodded, obviously exhausted.

"How did they find out the body is Angela Curry?"

"You know?"

"Yep, Steve Coleman told me."

"How did he get that information?" Ray said in an accusatory tone.

"Pamela Brown's podcast."

"The scandal reporter? New Hope PD hasn't even notified Angela's next of kin!"

"How do leaks usually get out? Someone on the inside, right?"

Ray scowled. Autumn knew that look. It was the face he made when running unsavory information through his mind; in this case, likely the list of staff members who knew about the situation.

"You've had a long day. Go change and wash up. Dinner is almost ready."

He left the room just as the pups finished their meal, and they ran after him. Autumn heard the delight in Ray's voice as he petted and played with them. The fur babies went a long way in helping him manage the stress of his job.

The three of them returned to the kitchen, Ray looking refreshed. Chrissy and Ace sat on either side of Ray's chair.

Autumn plated the meal of salmon, herbed rice, and mixed vegetables and put it on the table along with ice water. The food plus the dogs distracted Ray from his thoughts, and Autumn saw his body relax.

"Won't it be nice when you finally move in here for good?"

"It will. Only a couple of weeks more."

"Why wait until after the wedding?"

"We'd have waited another six months if we hadn't moved up the wedding date."

Autumn chewed her food and nodded.

"True, but these are modern times, after all. There's no rule that says you can't move in sooner."

"But there is a recent study that shows those who live together before marriage are more likely to divorce after the first year. Also, the quality of marriage is lower. I want our marriage to last forever, so let's give it the best chance we can."

"At least you didn't say you based it on some wedding superstition, like the groom can't see the bride before the wedding."

He took a bite of rice mixed with vegetables.

"Of course not. I'm a realist," said Ray, giving her a puzzled look.

"Bea told me that Saturday is the worst day to get married and that we should get married on a Wednesday for the best luck."

"How does that make sense?"

"Stacey Eldridge told her about wedding superstitions. She's worried that we'll be cursed if we don't abide by the rules."

Ray chuckled, and then shoveled the last of the salmon, rice, and veggies into his mouth. Autumn noticed that no matter what he ate, there was always an equal amount of each so he could mix them together and end his meal with all flavors.

"I pooh-poohed it, too. But then when I went to pick up our invitations at Tying the Knot, they were all wrong: the date, the font, your name."

"It's a coincidence. What are you going to do about the invitations?" Ray asked, wiping his mouth.

"Order them online. I'll never use that store for anything ever again and certainly won't recommend them."

"Do you want me to go talk to them?"

"No. I told her I wasn't paying for the cards. Brittany didn't seem to care, so I left."

"Brittany?"

"The owner of the shop."

"Whatever you think is best. If you need my help with anything, just ask."

"I know you're there when I need you." Autumn squeezed his hand. "I also have Bea and Elizabeth. I'm so lucky."

"It's not luck. It's because you're always there for everyone else. People love you, so they're there for you." Ray smiled lovingly at her.

"I'm still sad that my parents can't be there."

"Even though I don't know what to believe about the afterlife, I have a feeling that you'll feel their love on our wedding day."

"And your parents will be there. I really like them."

"They love you. Mom said she can't believe someone finally reeled me in."

"You never had a serious relationship before?"

"I lived with someone years ago out of convenience. Her name was Patty. It didn't work out."

Autumn fought back a pang of jealousy.

"Why not?"

"She was jealous and possessive. We had the definitive toxic relationship. I couldn't take it anymore."

"Where is she now?"

"No idea. I blocked her and moved on."

Autumn sensed he had nothing more to offer her on this topic.

"Well, I'm glad it worked out in my favor. How about some pumpkin pie and decaf coffee?"

"Let's have it in front of the fire."

"I'll get it. Take the pups in with you."

The four-legged family members leaped to attention when Ray stood, and followed him into the den.

Autumn wondered why Ray had never mentioned Patty before. Like he said, he'd moved on. In the same way, he never talked about his time in the service. When he moves on, he doesn't focus on it. She put whipped cream on the slices of pie and poured the fresh-brewed decaf. Autumn expertly balanced a loaded tray and brought it into the den.

The three of them, sitting on the floor near the fire, lifted her heart. Chrissy snuggled against Ray's leg, his left hand resting on her little body and his right rubbing Ace's head. A life filled with wonderful moments like this to cherish was more than she could ask for.

The smell of pie reached the dogs, and they came over to the coffee table.

"No, this isn't for you." She reached in her pocket and gave them each a jerky treat, which they greedily took and found a spot to enjoy it.

Ray settled onto the couch and took a plate. He closed his eyes as the pie and whipped cream melted in his mouth, then took a sip of coffee before saying, "This is so good!"

Autumn smiled. "I got the pie from Lisa Coleman's café. She makes the best."

Lisa, the daughter of Autumn's neighbor Steve Coleman, had made a name for herself since opening her café.

Ray finished his dessert in a few more bites, wiped his mouth, and washed it down with more coffee.

"You're the best," he said to Autumn.

"I try."

He waited a couple of beats, his expression turning serious.

"The wound on Angela Curry's body bothers me. I've never seen anything like it. The way it's shaped. We found no weapon near the body. The coroner said she was likely in that snow drift since around nine o'clock last night."

"It was definitely dark by that time and no one hangs out on that part of Main Street that late at night in the cold."

"Her office is across the street from where Chrissy found her." Chrissy's head lifted from her paws at the sound of her name. Ray petted her until she lay back down. "It could have happened when she closed her office for the evening."

"What about her patients? Who was the last one to leave last night?"

"They'll need to subpoena the records from the attorney who comes to close her office and secure her files. I don't think New Hope detectives got that far yet."

They sat in silence, listening to the crackling fire. Ray looked at his watch.

"It's getting late. Ace and I need to get going before I fall asleep."

"I can't wait until you don't have to leave."

"Me, too."

4

Autumn, Chrissy, Bea, and Stephanie Douglas, Autumn's best friend and maid of honor, rode in Stephanie's car into Center City, Philadelphia, to the bridal shop called With This Ring. The owner, Megan Harris, was an expert with antique wedding gowns and agreed to clean the gown Bea had found in the attic.

They parked in a garage a few doors down from the shop. Chrissy started sniffing as soon as Autumn put her down. The city had unfamiliar smells, and Chrissy took them all in. Head down, she found a little patch of grass to relieve herself before going into the bridal shop.

The pink and cream walls served as a backdrop to racks of sparkling gowns. Bea carried the gown in a zippered garment bag. A woman came from the back of the store wearing a pink suit, diamond broach on the lapel, and her gray hair done in a chignon bun. Her broad smile was warm and welcoming.

"Hello, ladies and furry darling." Chrissy wagged her tail. "I'm Megan Harris, owner of this establishment. How may I help you?"

"I'm Autumn Clarke. I called about the antique wedding dress."

"Oh, yes!" She walked over to Bea, took the garment bag, and hung it on a clear rack. "Let's have a look."

She unzipped the bag and let out a squeal of pleasure. "Fabulous!" Megan peeled the rest of the covering away and stood back to take it in. The ivory silk wedding gown had short flounce sleeves, and bugle beads that formed a starburst pattern, starting at the center and casting out to the edges of the gown. The beading continued on the train, making it sparkle.

"Okay to put her down?"

"Yes," said Megan.

Chrissy walked over to the gown and sniffed it. She put her paw on the garment bag, making a crinkling sound, and put her nose in it for a moment.

Autumn watched her carefully to ensure her safety, and that she was on her best behavior in the store.

"I'm hoping you can clean it and make sure all the beads are tight. I also need a veil or headpiece that complements the gown," Autumn asked.

"Yes, of course. When is the wedding?"

"December eleventh."

Bea sneered.

"Not much time, but we can make it work." She continued to admire the gown. "It's lovely, just lovely. It also satisfies the something old to signify your past. The headpiece is the something new to symbolize your future. For something blue, a garter that color will bring fidelity and love into the marriage." She pointed to the garter selection in a glass case. "Now all you need is something borrowed. It should be from someone happily married to bring you good fortune."

Autumn ran through the women in her life. The most happily married she among them was her mother. Other than that, most were divorced or single. "That might be a little tougher," she said.

"What about something from Ray's mom? His parents are happily married, right?" Stephanie offered.

"That's a good idea, Steph. And hopefully she'll feel more included."

"I'm glad that the old 'something old, something new, something borrowed, something blue' superstition is happening," said Bea with a knowing look.

Autumn smiled at her persistence.

"We'll also need two gowns. One for my maid of honor, Stephanie, and one for my stand-in for mother-of-the-bride, my cousin, Bea."

Bea took a step back.

"Really? I... I... I don't know what to say. I'm so honored!" Bea hugged Autumn.

"Absolutely. You're an important part of the family. Thanks for accepting." Autumn turned to Megan. "Whatever they want to wear is fine. It's on me."

"Right over here, ladies." Megan took them into a separate room with wedding party attire. "We probably need to stick with what's in stock, since time is short. Those gowns are on these racks." Megan pointed the way.

Bea and Stephanie combed through the racks, discussing colors and how their gowns might coordinate. They tried engaging Autumn for her opinion.

"Whatever you decide is fine. Seriously." Autumn giggled at their excitement.

"Last, but never least, is my flower girl, Chrissy." Autumn lifted her to eye level with Megan. "I'd like something for her that she won't try to shake off. And if she tries, it will stay on her. At least through the ceremony."

"I have just the thing. It's surprising how many pets people include in wedding ceremonies these days."

Autumn hugged Chrissy and gave her a kiss.

"They're part of the family, after all."

Megan walked over to a case that housed embellishments for dog collars.

"I like the one with pink satin roses with tulle attached. It looks like a little veil," said Autumn. She showed Chrissy, who smelled it and grunted.

"You can put it on her regular collar."

"That works out well, since her collar is already pink with rhinestones. Pink is her signature color."

Megan smiled. "Now, for your veil." She led Autumn to a wall of options. "We'll likely need to go with an in-stock item, as well."

"Do you think a veil is the best idea, or would a headpiece with beads look better?" Autumn asked.

"Did you know the veil wards off jealous spirits? And wearing a circle of flowers or beads also protects from evil spirits. We could do both; attach a short veil to a circle of beads similar to your gown."

"That sounds like a good option. All I'm hearing about are wedding superstitions lately. I'm not convinced that these precautions are necessary."

"Maybe unnecessary, but recommended. There's no harm in it. Why take the chance?" Megan chuckled and looked at the wall calendar. "You're getting married on a Saturday, too. English folklore says that's an unlucky day."

"My cousin Bea said the same thing. She said Wednesday is better."

"She's correct."

"Well, I have to re-order my invitations, so I could always change the date. I own the venue, so that's not a problem. It's just the guests being available."

"Re-order your invitations?"

Autumn explained what happened to the first order. Megan shook her head in disappointment.

"That's a shame. Well, let's make sure everything else goes as planned, shall we?"

She took down a beaded circle headpiece. The bugle beads matched the gown perfectly, and it fit Autumn's head.

"We can attach the veil here," Megan showed her the spot, "And match the color to the ivory of the gown."

"Sold," said Autumn.

Bea and Stephanie came rushing, in holding several gowns they wanted to try on. Megan got them set-up in dressing rooms, and Autumn sat on the sofa to watch the fashion show. Stephanie looked amazing in a beaded lavender form-fitting gown. Bea was perfect in a silver-gray long-sleeved gown with beaded lace across the bodice and down the sheer sleeves. It fit Bea's style and looked perfect on her.

They decided to wear simple beaded barrettes in their hair and selected two from the glass case. Only minor alterations were necessary, and the seamstress pinned the dresses for them, promising that they'd be ready when Autumn came to pick up her gown and headpiece.

Autumn wrote a check for fifty percent of the cost and they left the store beaming and chattered about their finds all the way home.

❄ ❄ ❄

Megan dialed the number from memory, as she had many times over the years, though she hated herself for doing so. But she couldn't blame anyone except herself. Accepting money for information about her customers was one thing; being blackmailed was another.

Mismanaging the shop finances put her on the verge of bankruptcy, making her vulnerable to the predator she now called. She still didn't know how the person found out about Megan's practice of overcharging customers' credit cards. Megan wondered if saving her business was enough of a reason for losing her integrity and harming others during what should be their happiest moments.

The phone connected.

"I have it," Megan said. She listened, then responded, "Uh, huh. Yes. Okay."

She hung up with a deep sigh, feeling slimy and heartsick.

5

Autumn, Bea, Stephanie, and Chrissy stopped at the Peabody Mansion on the way home, for a meeting with two people: Elizabeth Johnson, the B&B's decorator and event planner; and the inn's assistant manager, Kim Stokes. Autumn noticed Kim's heightened mood and motivation since her recent promotion from housekeeper to assistant manager, confirming Autumn's instincts were right.

Kim wore a burgundy cardigan over a graphic tee with a burst of color in the same family as the sweater and black jeans. They were all in casual mode until the inn officially opened in January.

Elizabeth had her hair styled in pom-poms, her go-to look when she was in creative mode. Her cream and denim-blue striped sweater looked stunning against her dark skin. Dangling bead earrings completed the look. Autumn envied her sense of style and ability to make jewelry. She wondered where Elizabeth found the time.

Chrissy squirmed in Autumn's arms, wanting to get down. The moment Autumn released her, she ran over to Elizabeth and Kim, wagging her tail. They both knelt to greet her with enthusiastic rubs and high-pitched compliments of being so beautiful and such a good girl. Chrissy ate it up.

"Come here, sweetheart," Autumn called. "It's too warm in here to wear your coat."

Chrissy trotted over to Autumn, let her remove her jacket, and shook out her hair.

"Hi, ladies," said Elizabeth, now able to acknowledge the others in the room. Queen Chrissy always came first.

"Check out the plan for the wedding!" Kim exclaimed. "Elizabeth outdid herself."

They gathered around the table where the idea board and glittering samples covered the surface.

"Since not everyone on the guest list celebrates Christmas, we're going with a winter theme, showcasing sparkling snowflakes and icicles hanging from the ceiling, Snow Queen fairy-tale ornaments on the ten-foot artificial tree flecked with snow and white twinkle lights will stand in the corner of the living room, white tablecloths made from iridescent fabric..." Elizabeth exclaimed, before Kim interrupted her.

"Isn't it fabulous?" she said, rubbing her hands together. "Absolutely magical!"

Elizabeth smiled at her biggest fan.

Chrissy let out one sharp bark. Autumn lifted her so she could see, too. She wagged her tail in approval.

"We can also leave these decorations up for the grand opening in January," said Elizabeth, "minus the ice sculpture for the food table. I called Harry Halifax, the best ice sculptor in the area. He suggested a wedding tree with yours and Ray's initials carved into the trunk."

"It's going to be really beautiful," Autumn said, while Bea and Stephanie nodded. "Maybe we can use this theme for the new wedding invitations."

"I thought you ordered them and picked them up," Stephanie said, frowning.

"Forgot to tell you. They were completely wrong. The date, Ray's name. It was horrible. I left them at Tie the Knot. Please don't refer any business to them."

"No worries there!" said Stephanie.

"I think it's a sign. We need to change the date of the wedding," said Bea, sticking with her cursed-wedding theory.

"Why?" Kim said, confused

"Saturday is bad luck. Wednesday is better," said Bea.

"I'd have to take off work. School doesn't break for the holidays until the week before Christmas," said Stephanie, who taught fifth grade at Knollwood Elementary School.

Autumn said nothing, but gazed at Bea, her point made.

"Then we'll need to be careful to ensure good luck."

"Like what?" Elizabeth had her notepad ready to write any requirements.

Autumn couldn't wait to hear what else Bea had in mind, given Stacey Eldridge's advice.

"For one thing, we need to ring bells during the ceremony to keep evil spirits away. It's an Irish tradition." She glanced at Autumn.

Autumn didn't want to sound ungrateful for Bea's desire to bring as much good luck and protection as possible, and her family name of Clarke had Irish heritage, despite discovering she was a

Peabody, whose origins were English. She was skeptical about the effect of the bells, but figured it couldn't hurt.

"They need to be gentle-sounding bells, otherwise it might scare Chrissy," said Autumn, knowing her pup's reaction to sudden or loud noises.

Elizabeth suggested, "Let me look into it."

"We'll also need a bell in the bridal bouquet," said Bea, tapping Elizabeth's notepad. "And no yellow roses! They symbolize jealousy."

Elizabeth was in charge of making the bouquet, so she jotted it down.

"Aren't they a sign of friendship and new beginnings?" asked Stephanie, pretty sure that's what most people believed.

"Not in Victorian times. Better not to take the chance," Bea replied.

Stephanie shrugged.

"Got it," Elizabeth affirmed.

Bea nodded and crossed her arms. "Good."

"Elizabeth, would you mind ordering the invitations? I trust your judgment."

"Sure. I'll get them online. I have a speedy printer I use. We'll have them within two days."

"Thank you," said Autumn, picking up Chrissy. "Now to get hold of Sarah."

Sarah Kelly, a graduate of The Restaurant School in Philadelphia, was the new chef for the Peabody Mansion Bed and Breakfast.

"You're having Sarah cater the wedding and not Lisa Coleman?"

"I want Lisa to have fun as a guest, not have to work that day. But don't worry, as a wedding gift, she's making all the desserts, except for the wedding cake."

Kim and Elizabeth grinned broadly and rubbed their hands together.

"Can't wait for that!" said Kim.

Autumn knew they were excited about being guests at the wedding and seemed even more charged up to eat whatever Lisa Coleman had in mind.

"I put an order in last week for the cake at Annabella's in New Hope," Elizabeth told the others. "And then the oddest thing happened. I called yesterday to go over some details, and

Annabella said she got a call saying that we canceled the wedding, so no cake. I told her to put us back on the schedule and told her how to decorate it."

Bea's mouth started to open and Autumn jumped in.

"We're not cursed, Bea! But something is going on."

❄ ❄ ❄

Harry Halifax focused on his latest creation, a three-foot nutcracker for the reception following a performance of The Nutcracker at The Academy of Music. Board members, local CEOs, and wealthy supporters of the arts would be there to witness his latest work of art and hopefully take a business card from holders positioned at the reception desk.

His breath made clouds as he worked in the cold, chipping away at the block of ice, tools sharp and gleaming. Two decades of working in this medium made him an expert in producing any shape for any occasion. Harry had the honor of working all over the world on special projects. It also gave him time away from his wife, Faith, allowing his female admirers to spend some time with him. He always came home to her, no matter how good his trysts made him feel. If Faith suspected anything, she never said.

Despite his preference for these relationships to take place far from his home in New Hope, there was one local sexual escapade he just couldn't resist—Angela Curry. He'd met her during a creative slump, hoping therapy would help him get back into the zone. The effect her technique had on him made him come back for more, even after he regained his motivation. And, like the others, Faith didn't know he was in therapy nor that he got his fixes outside the marital bed so close to home. Even though Angela was Harry's newfound inspiration, and he sculpted Angela's beautiful body in ice, he told Faith he made it for a plastic surgeon's office. Angela kept him in bliss until he told her it was time to end their sessions.

No other woman reacted the way Angela had: screaming at him, threatening to tell his wife, and ending his career. He was the last patient she saw the night before they found her body the next day. A body that he had sculpted early on. Angela made him so mad. And now she was dead and his worries were over.

❄ ❄ ❄

26

Beatrice went over to the Peabody Museum side of the building to pick Stacey's brain a bit more about safeguarding the wedding. Stephanie, Autumn, Chrissy, and Elizabeth took a walk down the cold, white trail, past the snow-covered, life-sized statuary of fairies, gargoyles, buddhas from various cultures, and pagodas along the trail and nestled in the woods, to the clearing where the ancient sycamore stood surrounded by snowdrifts and lit by the hazy glimmer of trail lights buried in snow.

"I suggest we change out some of the statues. Gargoyles were great for Halloween, but not for a wedding," said Elizabeth.

Stephanie agreed.

Autumn said, "You two can pick out whatever you think is best. I trust your judgment. You've got your work cut out for you, Elizabeth."

"I'll get Ward to help me clear the path and lights, lay down some fresh pea gravel, replace the statues, and put up the chairs."

Ward Everly was the handyman turned permanent groundskeeper who'd built the hay bale maze for the Halloween extravaganza. Ward's mysterious presence and seemingly endless talents made him a wonderful addition to the staff, despite his odd ways. He had a peculiar habit of turning up when you didn't know anyone was near, moving quietly indoors and out. Ward had a unique sense of vigilante justice that Autumn and her staff somehow found comforting. He had a protective way about him and got along with everyone on the team. Even Chrissy liked him, and she was an excellent judge of character.

"This is such a beautiful spot to get married," said Stephanie. "The bushes and trees around this clearing break the wind and doesn't feel as cold as it does out on the driveway."

"In addition to the gas heaters, we'll be putting up a fabric barrier around the site, including around the chairs, to keep folks as warm as possible," Elizabeth explained.

"Brilliant! As usual," Autumn clapped her on the back.

"Won't the heaters look too industrial?" worried Stephanie.

"We'll camouflage them with flowers and greenery, with the heating element sticking out of the top to get a romantic look," Elizabeth assured her.

Stephanie smiled and nodded.

Autumn noticed Chrissy shaking with cold, even with her heavy winter coat. She picked her up and stuffed her inside her thick jacket so that her head stuck out.

"You're the cutest flower girl ever," Stephanie said, stroking Chrissy's ears. "We'll make sure you're comfortable for the ceremony, little one."

Twilight descended over the trail. Autumn could picture the magical atmosphere Elizabeth planned to create for the wedding. She hoped their luck would hold out, despite the attempts to sabotage her invitations and cake.

6

Pamela Brown typed the last few sentences on her latest gossip column and sat back, satisfied. The story about Angela Curry was sure to increase subscribers to her podcast and her website. Angela's reputation in the community was spotless, but that was about to change.

Since her murder, the community speculated about who could have killed her, but no one knew where to look for suspects, not even the police. But Pamela knew there were many viable people with reasons to eliminate her. As the area's busiest therapist, Angela had dirt on pretty much everyone, much of which she spoon-fed to Pamela. Such a tease with information, but Pamela took whatever she could get and surmised the rest.

Angela's patients did not know they were opening their deepest thoughts and emotional pain to a woman who was ready to expose them for the right price. Pamela already missed her best source of information, but she'd get one last bit from Ms. Curry once they found the murderer. That would be the story of the year.

Angela's death was a significant loss to her information stream. Pamela added a line at the end of her blog post, asking anyone with information to contact her.

In the meantime, her living sources fed her information about the investigation and an upcoming wedding—that of Knollwood Police Lieutenant Raymond Reed and his fiancé, heiress Autumn Clarke Peabody. Her inheritance from the famous local family she didn't know she was related to until recently and her friendship with movie star Dana Wood made for great gossip, and listeners ate it up. Now, word on the street was that the wedding may not go forward. They had canceled the wedding cake, so there may be trouble in paradise. Pamela vowed to get to the bottom of it.

❊ ❊ ❊

"Any news about the Curry case?" asked William Moore, a detective with the New Hope Police Department. He cradled the phone against his ear and took notes as he listened to the pathologist's report.

Angela Curry had an unusual hole in her chest in the shape of a V. It was deep and penetrated her heart, but there was no murder weapon nearby, and very little blood. The puncture didn't fit a knife wound signature, or even a screwdriver for that matter. So, was it a tool? With a workshop loaded with a variety of tools for woodworking, repairing, and building, Detective Moore couldn't think of one shaped in a V. Time of death was around nine o'clock the night before they'd found the body.

William Moore was there when they dug out Angela Curry's body from the snowdrift. He also kept an eye on Autumn Clarke and her little dog, Chrissy, when they stood with Lieutenant Ray Reed watching the activity. He'd first seen her at the festival when her pup found the skeletal remains of a body in the ground. Her auburn hair draped over her shoulders and perfect figure attracted him right away. He moved to introduce himself, but Ray Reed and his German shepherd, Ace, came and stood guard. So, he watched from the sidelines as she cuddled her pup, wishing it could be him in her arms.

William's interactions with people during his decade-long law enforcement career gave him the ability to quickly assess people. Autumn was a rare person who exuded love and intelligence. Since then, he'd attempted to get close to her by going to the Peabody Museum, hoping to run into her. Those brief conversations with her showed him that not only was she loving and smart but also loyal, especially to Ray Reed. The only way he had a chance with her was if Autumn and Ray called off the wedding.

Detective Moore scowled. Would Autumn's interest turn toward him if she didn't have Ray in her life? She was always friendly to him, but could that turn into a relationship?

He tucked the notepad into a roomy pocket of his coat, turning his thoughts to the case and away from the image of Autumn's smiling face.

❄ ❄ ❄

Faith Halifax put away her husband's ice sculpting tools and cleaned up his studio. As the wife of an artist, she was careful not to disrupt the space and so interrupt his creative flow. She always thought that his philandering was part of his artistic process, so said nothing about Harry's many affairs. She didn't mind as much when it happened far from home, but when she found the text from Angela Curry saying she planned to run away with Harry, that was the last straw.

She noticed a difference in him after he'd started therapy with Angela. He thought Faith didn't know, but between the insurance paperwork, which she took care of, and following him to Angela's office, she knew his desperation to rekindle his creativity drove him to therapy. And when the relationship shifted from therapy to something more personal, Faith could tell they were sleeping together because he was less demanding in the marital bed.

He sculpted an image of Angela and told her it was an idealized image for a plastic surgeon's grand opening, but Faith knew better. Harry made an ice sculpture of Faith early in their relationship. She knew the drill and the way his highs and lows affected his work. He chose subjects that were close to his heart at that moment, unless otherwise instructed by a client.

When she heard about that little Shih Tzu discovering Angela's body, Faith grinned, knowing that her marriage was no longer threatened.

She vigorously rubbed the ten-inch chipper tool with its V-shaped blade until it gleamed. She wondered why it was in his delivery truck. Maybe he brought it for last-minute touchups. He had made a local delivery to a business on Main Street soon after the finding of the body. But that didn't explain the dull streaks that covered the tool. Faith had been expertly caring for Harry's tools over the years, sometimes fantasizing about using them on him or his latest conquest for embarrassing her. But then he'd give her attention, placating her until the next time.

Humming to herself, Faith placed the tool in its case and put it in line with the other razor-sharp tools of the trade.

❄ ❄ ❄

Elizabeth met with Harry Halifax in his office, going through photos of various tree designs and showing him her vision board for the event. Harry's artistic ability impressed her, and her excitement at working with him had her talking a mile a minute. Their proximity made Elizabeth want to move even closer to him. There was a certain sex appeal about artists she found irresistible. But Harry's marriage made him off limits; she wouldn't intrude on that sacred bond.

Even so, she jumped away from him when the office door opened and Harry's wife, Faith, entered, giving a knowing smile and greeting Elizabeth.

"Thanks for using Harry for the wedding event of the season," Faith said.

"It's actually smaller than you'd expect. Autumn and Ray prefer intimate gatherings."

"Still, I'm sure the society pages online and in print will carry the story and lots of photos."

"We'll make sure the sculpture gets its deserved publicity. And, of course, his business cards will be available," Elizabeth assured her.

Harry smiled and reached out to Faith, beckoning her closer. He wrapped an arm around her waist and showed the plan to her.

"They're getting married under a sycamore tree, so the sculpture will reflect that species in winter. I'm inspired to imagine how it fits into Elizabeth's design. It may be one of my best pieces yet," he said.

Faith pressed against him. "I'm sure they'll love it. Your tools are all clean and organized."

"Thanks, my love," he said and kissed her on the lips. "What would I do without you?"

"Let's not find out, eh?" said Faith, as she waved goodbye to Elizabeth and left.

≈ 7 ≈

Autumn bundled up Chrissy, placed her in the car seat, and topped her with a soft pink blanket, tucking it around her. Chrissy sighed and rested her chin on the edge of the car seat, facing her mommy. Autumn gazed at her cute little furry bundle, forever amazed at how Chrissy preferred watching her drive rather than to look out the window.

They backed out of the garage and onto the street, bordered with piles of snow, a reminder of the body. Autumn allowed her mind to wander, wondering how many other bodies could be buried along the side of the road. Chrissy let out one sharp bark, bringing Autumn back to the present.

"What is it, sweetheart?" Autumn asked, petting Chrissy's head without taking her eyes off the road.

The streets looked free of snow and ice, but the chance of a slippery spot made Autumn drive with caution.

Chrissy moved to get out of her car seat.

"No, you can't sit on my lap."

The pup occasionally tried to wiggle onto Autumn's lap, but it would be dangerous for her if, God forbid, they were in an accident and the airbag deployed.

Chrissy sat back down.

"We'll be there in a few minutes."

Judge Terri Cromwell lived in New Hope, near where Chrissy had found Angela Curry's body. Judge Cromwell invited them to her home to discuss the wedding ceremony. Stephanie met them there to provide her valued opinion on the vows and ceremony details.

Autumn found a parking spot on the side street where the Judge's house stood among other narrow three-story dwellings, each painted in different muted shades of blue, green, gray, and white. Autumn loved the charm of the town and the friendly vibe expressed by passersby as they bent down to pet Chrissy.

They found an open patch of snowy ground for Chrissy to squat on before knocking on Judge Cromwell's door. The sound of the heavy doorknocker echoed through the house. Quick footsteps clicked along the hard floor. The Judge opened the door and welcomed them in. Judge Cromwell wore slacks and a sweater, the layers of short dark hair neatly combed into place.

"There's that smart little girl," she said, ruffling Chrissy's hair. Chrissy shook, putting her hair back into place, and wagged her tail.

She had a hug for Autumn, a handshake for Stephanie, and took their coats, including Chrissy's. Autumn lifted Chrissy off the floor and pulled a mini towel from Chrissy's go-bag to wipe her feet as the judge showed them into the living room just off the foyer.

"She's fine. A little dampness won't hurt anything."

For Chrissy's benefit, Autumn made sure Chrissy's paws were dry and salt-free before putting her down. Chrissy explored the room with her nose before sitting on the floor next to her mommy.

"Thanks for meeting with us on your day off, Judge." Autumn said.

"Of course! I'm excited about the big day. And please call me Terri."

"It was so nice of Megan to refer me to you."

"She told me about that gorgeous antique gown of yours. In all the years she's had the bridal shop, she's never seen anything like it."

"It's definitely unique," said Stephanie.

"My cousin found it in the attic of the Peabody Mansion. I'm fortunate that it fits me. There's so much cool stuff up there."

Footsteps pounded down the stairs. A dark-haired male in his late teens with Terri's features came into the doorway. He wore his torn jeans low with a gray sweatshirt imprinted in forest green with the words Tree Crest and an oak tree icon beneath it.

Chrissy walked over to the teen and sniffed his hiking boots, jerking her head back suddenly as if getting a whiff of something she didn't like. She started barking at him.

"I'm so sorry," said Autumn, moving to grab Chrissy.

Terri pressed her lips together before she spoke in a clipped tone. "This is my son, Barry. Barry, this is Autumn, Stephanie, and Chrissy," pointing to each in turn. "I'm officiating her wedding."

"The woman or the dog?" Barry smirked before walking down the hall.

Terri's face reddened.

"I apologize for my son's rudeness," she said, her eyes slits of frustration.

"And for Chrissy's reaction. I don't know what got into her."

"He has that effect on most dogs. I guess they don't like his energy. Most times, neither do I." Terri shook her head sadly.

Chrissy squirmed in Autumn's arms. Autumn held Chrissy close and stroked her head, trying to calm her.

Stephanie sat in stunned silence.

"I'll get her some water," said Terri, following her son down the hall.

Chrissy whined in Autumn's arms.

"It's okay, sweetheart."

Autumn was putting Chrissy's coat on by the time Terri returned with a bowl of water and put it on the floor, but Chrissy turned her head. Stephanie already had herself bundled up to go out into the cold.

"I'm so sorry to cut our meeting short, but Chrissy is too agitated for us to have a productive meeting. I'll email you the vows and we can find a date for you to come to the inn to walk through the ceremony."

"That sounds good. Sorry for the disruption."

"No problem. Everything will work out as it should."

Terri reached out to pet Chrissy goodbye, but she let out one bark and turned toward the door.

"I'll see you soon," said Terri.

Autumn nodded.

"Nice meeting you, Stephanie."

"Same here."

Outside, they saw Terri's son up ahead, trudging toward Main Street. He must have exited the house through a back door. A woman held her French bulldog's leash tight, as it barked and snarled at Barry as he walked by, ignoring the dog.

"Wow, such terrible energy," said Stephanie.

Autumn felt sorry for Barry. His inability to win the love of dogs was a true curse. Was his connection to Terri and her role in their wedding part of the curse Beatrice was so worried about?

⚡ 8 ⚡

A laminated sign hung on the door of Angela Curry's office, instructing clients to call Jodi Fallston for important information.

Ray knocked on the door before turning the knob to enter. A woman in a gray business suit sat at the desk, staring at a laptop screen, piles of files surrounding her. She looked up.

"May I help you?" she asked in a smooth voice that took charge of the conversation.

"I'm Lieutenant Reed. I'm investigating the murder of Ms. Curry and hoping you can help me."

She pointed to a chair opposite her.

"Have a seat. I'm Jodi Fallston, the PE for this case."

Ray sat. "PE?"

"Professional Executor and Angela's attorney."

"Looks like you have your hands full."

"Closing a psychologist's office tends to be labor intensive for me, and emotional for patients. They worry their files will fall into the wrong hands and are reluctant to engage with a new doctor. For me, it's about ensuring the cataloging, confidentiality, and safe transfer of files while executing the Professional Will."

"Sounds like your role is critical to the wellbeing of Ms. Curry's patients."

"Which is why I have a psychologist Angela designated in the will contacting her patients and taking them on or reassigning them."

"She had someone already named?"

"Sure. Psychotherapists have an ethical and legal duty to plan for just such contingency in the event of their sudden death."

"Do you know if Angela was afraid of any of her patients? Did she feel threatened?"

"Not that she mentioned."

"When did you speak with her last?"

Jodi pulled out her cell phone, tapped it, and looked at her calendar.

"Last Tuesday."

"Were there any updates to the will during that conversation?"

"No."

"I understand about patient confidentiality, but we're trying to gather information that could lead us to Ms. Curry's murderer. Can you give us the name of the last patient she saw the night she was killed?"

Jodi turned to the laptop and searched for information.

"Her patients all signed a HIPAA paper about disclosure of certain information. It stipulates that we can share information with police pertaining to a criminal investigation. So, yes."

A few more taps on the keyboard.

"Her last client was from eight to nine o'clock the evening of her death. The patient's name is Harry Halifax."

"The ice sculptor?"

"I believe so."

"Thank you very much, Ms. Fallston."

They shook hands. Ray took Jodi Fallston's card from the desk and handed her one of his.

Outside, he called Autumn as he walked to his SUV. She answered.

"What's the name of the ice sculptor we're using for our wedding?"

"Harry Halifax. Why?"

"Right now, he's a prime candidate for the murder of Angela Curry."

❄ ❄ ❄

Autumn hung up, a weight in her stomach at this next round of trouble in the wedding plans. Dare she tell Beatrice of yet another sign that a curse hung over their ceremony and celebration?

She got home and unloaded Chrissy from the car. Inside, Chrissy ran to the sliding door and looked at Autumn, who slid it open for her. Chrissy took off across the snowy patio, tinkled in her clearing, and then dove into a snow pile. Autumn closed the door to keep the heat in, as her ball of fur frolicked in the snow.

She stood watching Chrissy as she dialed Elizabeth's number.

"Hey, Autumn! I just had the best meeting with Harry Halifax and his wife. The sculpture is going to be fabulous!"

Autumn gulped.

"About that. Maybe we should expand our search for an ice sculptor."

"But Harry's the best and really gets our vision."

"There may be some complication about using him. Don't cancel just yet, but let's make sure we have a contingency plan."

No response.

"Did I lose you?"

"No."

Autumn heard the disappointment in Elizabeth's voice.

"Listen, trust me on this. I can't go into detail right now."

"Okay."

"Thanks. I'll keep you posted."

She disconnected the call as Chrissy pressed her nose against the glass. Autumn removed Chrissy's coat and grabbed the towel she kept by the back door, wrapping her baby in it, hugging and kissing her as she wiped the snow from her paws and legs. Chrissy grunted in her mommy's arms and licked Autumn's face.

"You're such a good girl!" Autumn said, giving Chrissy one last squeeze and putting her down. "No matter what, you always make me feel better."

Chrissy wagged her tail and ran over to her water bowl and lapped the cool, fresh water.

Autumn sat at the kitchen table, watching her. Chrissy had faced challenges in her brief life, but now she allowed herself to enjoy a loving environment. She set a good example for others, especially Autumn, to follow. No matter what difficulties she faced, she'd allow herself to focus on the blessings that surrounded her. Even if she married Ray with no one there besides two-and-four-legged immediate family, closest friends, and the big old sycamore tree, that would be good enough for her. No ice sculpture needed.

❄ ❄ ❄

Disappointment filled Elizabeth, but she knew Autumn wouldn't ask her to come up with another sculptor without good reason. Not one to waste time, she arrived at the Peabody Mansion to meet with Sarah Kelly, the inn's executive chef, to go over the menu.

Elizabeth had high standards for herself and those she worked with. In Elizabeth's mind, Sarah ranked at the top of the list of those who impressed her the most. Sarah was in the reception area chatting with Kim Stokes when Elizabeth arrived. Working with these two made her job easy. Both were reliable, dedicated, and fun to brainstorm with.

"Hey, ladies!"

They returned the greeting.

"Let's sit in the den to go over the menu," Elizabeth suggested.

They settled in and got down to business.

"I've made a preliminary menu and suggestions for drinks," said Sarah, distributing copies of her ideas.

"Ooh! The champagne and pear, apple, and blood orange nectar sound amazing," said Kim.

"We will center it in the reception area so that it's the first thing guests see and will allow them to get a drink. Elizabeth, do you think the ice sculptor can create an ice chute for the nectar so it's nice and cold when it hits the champagne?"

Elizabeth took a breath.

"I'll be sure to include that detail." She made a note, hoping she could fulfill the request.

"The butlered hors d'oeuvres are all vegetarian: meatless meatballs made with eggs, cheese and parsley smothered in tomato sauce, bruschetta on toasted bread. There's a gluten-free option available. Italian olive tapenade and spicy kale and white beans, and Arancini, which are rice balls stuffed with peas and tomato sauce."

"My stomach is rumbling just thinking about it," said Kim.

"I'm putting a food-preference section on the RSVP cards, so we'll know if anyone is gluten-free, dairy-free, or meat-free. So many dietary restrictions these days." said Elizabeth made another note.

"Let me know of any changes to the pasta station, too, please," said Sarah.

She pointed to the list of suggestions for three types of pasta that included campanelle, a wedding bell shaped pasta with homemade tomato sauce, sweet potato gnocchi with browned butter and sage, pasta with gorgonzola cream sauce, and pappardelle with Radicchio and Pancetta.

"The sit-down dinner includes a festive salad with champagne vinaigrette, Italian wedding soup, which we can change to vegetable based. If need be, I can make both. Then Caprese salad, chicken or crispy tofu marsala with Kennett Square mushrooms, cauliflower, and broccoli in extra virgin olive oil, capers, and garlic. For the meat eaters, I'll make braised short ribs or they can choose chicken saltimbocca al la Romana."

"Once we get all the RSVPs, we'll go over the number of servings of each option," said Elizabeth.

"Perfect. I understand Lisa is making the desserts," Sarah answered. "I've been to her café, and her raspberry tarts are a killer."

High praise from a graduate of The Restaurant School in Philadelphia.

"Agreed!" Kim said enthusiastically. She'd been a huge fan of Lisa's baked goods ever since the Halloween extravaganza.

"With dessert, I'm thinking we'll have a bar with coffee, espresso, herbal tea, sambuca, brandy, and homemade Limoncello. Also, a hot chocolate bar with lots of extras for guests to customize their drink."

"What if we served the hot chocolate and other warm beverages in the beginning, too, since guests are coming in from the cold after the ceremony?" suggested Elizabeth.

"Sure, we can do that." Sarah made a note.

"We'll display the cake on a table in the dining room, along with the other desserts." Sarah checked that item on her sheet. "Anything else?"

"I think we're covered," said Elizabeth.

"Do we need to meet with Autumn to finalize the menu?"

"No. She told me to surprise her. I swear, she must be the easiest bride-to-be in existence," Elizabeth said.

Kim cleared her throat. "But run it by Beatrice. She's pretty specific about how this wedding is organized. She trying to protect the wedding from a curse."

"Curse?" said Sarah.

"She said certain things have to be done to ensure good luck and happiness for the bride and groom."

Elizabeth chimed in, "Yeah, so far we've got ruined invitations and a canceled wedding cake."

Sarah looked horrified.

"Don't worry, I'm taking care of it, but it's set Beatrice on a mission to block the curse."

"Shall I speak with her, then?" asked Sarah.

"Let's schedule a meeting with the three of us, plus Beatrice. Then we'll make sure to cover all bases," said Elizabeth.

"Sounds like a plan," said Kim.

⚡ **9** ⚡

"Hello, Mrs. Reed. How are you?" Autumn telephoned her mother-in-law-to-be.

"Just fine, dear. I'm excited about the wedding," said Ray's mother, Carol. "And please call me Mom or Carol, whichever you prefer."

Autumn's heart lifted.

"I'd love to call you Mom! Thank you. It'll be so nice to have a mom again."

"It must be hard without her. She was so young. I'm no replacement, but I'm happy to have you as a daughter."

Autumn smiled ear-to-ear. "I'm honored," she said Atumn. "I know we're not related yet, but may I ask a favor?"

"Of course."

"We're upholding wedding traditions, and I need something borrowed. According to legend, it should be from someone in a happy marriage."

"How lovely! Now I'm honored. I have just the thing."

"This means a lot to me. Shall I come pick it up or would you like to come here? I'll make some hot chocolate. It's my mother's special recipe."

"Sold, plus it will give me practice getting to your place for when Ray moves in."

"Great, see you in a bit."

Autumn liked Carol Reed and looked forward to having her and her husband, Kevin, over for dinners and televised sports events. Ray loved watching *the game,* whichever one it was for the season. He yelled at the TV, but Autumn felt he'd enjoy it a lot more with his dad and maybe his best friend, Adam, there to watch it with him.

Adam was dating Autumn's best friend, Stephanie, so they could cook and chat in the kitchen with Carol while the men were in the den watching the game. The vision filled her heart with joy.

Carol Reed was at Autumn's house within the hour. Chrissy ran to the door and barked in her someone's-at-the-door tone. When Carol stepped over the threshold, Chrissy ran up to her, body swaying with her tail in welcome.

"There's that pretty girl!" Carol exclaimed, putting her purse and gift bag down to pet the length of the Shih Tzu. Chrissy patted her leg, so Carol scooped her up and snuggled her close, cooing, "That's my sweet little one."

A kiss to the head, and she put Chrissy down. Autumn came to her for a hug. Chrissy let out one bark and ran into the den. When Carol didn't follow, Chrissy came to the doorway and let out another bark.

Autumn laughed. "Better go with her. I think she wants to show you her toy pile. I'll put your things in the kitchen."

Autumn heard the squeak of Chrissy's favorite piggy toy and the sounds of Chrissy attacking the toy and Carol laughing. Autumn put the milk on the stove and started making the hot chocolate. She pulled down two large snowflake mugs and set them on the counter.

"Can I help?" Carol asked.

Chrissy walked past her to get a drink of water.

"I've got this. Have a seat and relax."

Carol sat in the chair that was Autumn's mother's favorite spot. Maybe it was fate. Autumn placed the mugs on the table, along with a bowl of miniature marshmallows and a spoon.

"That smells heavenly!" said Carol and took a sip before adding a spoonful of marshmallows.

Chrissy pawed Autumn's leg, and she lifted her fur baby onto her lap.

"It's nice having you here. I'm hoping we can see more of each other once the wedding madness is over."

"Kevin and I are ready for that. We don't see much of Ray with his work schedule. Before that, his last girlfriend wasn't too keen on including us in their lives."

"He told me they lived together."

"Yes, and she barred us from visiting them and refused to come to our house. Patty was very possessive."

"Ray doesn't seem the type to tolerate that."

"He's not. He was always independent, even as a child."

"I plan to take care of him and that includes you and Mr. Reed."

"If you're going to call me Mom, then you can call him Pop, like Ray does."

"Okay. I like the sound of that."

42

"You're a much better fit for him, dear. He's calm and happy since meeting you."

"I feel the same way. And Chrissy and Ace being friends makes me happy, too."

Carol pushed the small purple glittery gift bag over to Autumn.

"If this is the *something borrowed*, then it's not a gift, right?"

"Right."

Autumn shuffled through the tissue paper and found a weighty item wrapped in more tissue. She unrolled it.

"A bride and groom statuette! They look so in love."

The groom wore a black tuxedo. The bride held a bouquet of pink flowers and wore a white sleeveless dress. They faced each other, lovingly looking into each other's eyes. The groom held her around the waist and her hand was on his shoulder as they lean in for a kiss.

"It was the cake topper from our wedding."

Autumn put Chrissy down and hugged Carol tight.

"I love it. How special. I'll put it in a safe place and put it on the cake before it's displayed."

Autumn re-wrapped it carefully and put it back in the bag.

"Do you have your dress yet?" Autumn asked.

"I do. It's iridescent beige with turquoise beading."

"Can't wait to see it. I need to pick up my dress in a couple of days. Want to take a ride?"

"Just let me know when."

Ward Everly, the groundskeeper and self-designated protector of Autumn and all associated with her, came out from the woodland trail at the Peabody Mansion. He put his heart and soul into making the approach to the sycamore tree safe and warm for wedding guests. The shoveling he did today may have to be done again if another storm came. Locals could likely get home if it snowed again. Out-of-town guests were staying at the inn, anyway. No matter, he'd make sure everything was ready.

His broad shoulders and specially outfitted dolly moved the gargoyle statuary from Halloween into the woods to protect the area. Guests couldn't see them, but he figured their energy worked just as well in the woods as it did on the path. He was more suspicious than superstitious, but he figured it couldn't hurt. He heard about some of the stuff going on with the wedding plans. It stunk of sabotage to him, but he'd stay vigilant.

Elizabeth thought the gargoyles looked too menacing and replaced them with Chinese goddesses that looked more appropriate for the occasion. The five-foot tall statues all had specific meanings to help the couple start their lives together on a high note. They included Quan Yin, the goddess of love, peace, and compassion, Nuwa the creator goddess called on for fertility, and Lady Xian, a protective goddess. Working around this place educated him in all kinds of things he'd never known before. With the fertility goddess at the ceremony, he hoped Ray and Autumn wanted children. They'd make great parents, and he'd look forward to building them a playhouse with swings and slides.

He overheard a conversation between Beatrice and Elizabeth regarding the statues. Beatrice insisted that the path have foo dogs guarding the entrance, one on either side, to protect the couple and bring them good fortune. She was very specific about their placement: the female on the left and the male on the right. He thought they both looked the same until she pointed out that the male had a ball under his paw and the female had a puppy under hers. Hence, Elizabeth switched from Roman goddesses to Chinese goddesses to go with the foo dog theme.

Ward was all for protecting the happy couple, so he was fine with it and installed them as instructed. Besides, he didn't want to tangle with Beatrice. She could be tough. At the same time, he admired her dedication to Autumn.

He enjoyed working with Elizabeth. She had a good head on her shoulders and fit in well with the others who worked at the Peabody Mansion. They shared a bond that was easy and caring. This was the first time he felt like he belonged, especially since Ray and Autumn invited him to the wedding as a guest, not a worker.

Ward looked toward the front door of the mansion. There was a medium-sized, brown cardboard box on the steps. Odd, since he didn't hear a delivery truck. When he walked over to the door, he saw that the label said *To Ray and Autumn*. There was no *from* written on there. Maybe there was a card inside the box. He listened to the box before picking it up. They'd had fishy deliveries before with intent to harm, so he took the side of caution. Quiet. He didn't want Autumn to open it alone. He hit Autumn's number and told her about the situation.

"I'll send Ray over, and the two of you can open it. He can decide if we need further action. Hopefully, it's just an early wedding present."

Ward hoped she was right.

Ray arrived. Ward had a box cutter ready to slice through the brown duct tape on the outside of the box. Inside was a wooden box. They lifted it out and opened the latch. Three thick-bladed knives with heavy wooden handles were nestled inside, their silver heads gleaming. No card was underneath it or inside of it.

Beatrice pulled up and saw them hovering over the box. She hurried over.

"Knives! Who are they from?" she shouted.

"Looks like an early wedding gift," said Ray. "No card, so I don't know who they're from."

"Get rid of them! They're bad luck!"

She reached for the box. Ray held her back.

"Why would someone do that?"

"If you don't mind me saying, somebody has a beef about this wedding. Weird things have been happening. I'm with Beatrice on this one. These are no ordinary knives. They are hand-forged, professional blades. They can cut through anything," said Ward.

"Right! They signify a broken relationship. Someone sending a message that they want your relationship to end."

"I see it as a threat, too, Ray," said Ward.

Ray groaned. "Is this the curse idea again?"

"Don't make fun. Better safe than sorry," begged Bea. She grabbed her phone from her purse and dialed Autumn, explaining the situation and ending with, "I want to get them out of here. Don't even bring them into the mansion or your house."

She listened to Autumn's response and then said, "Okay."

"Autumn said since we don't know who it's from and it could be an oversight, don't throw them away. Put them in the storage shed and see if anyone claims the gift being from them."

"I'll take care of that," Ward offered, happy to be part of the solution.

Beatrice was shaking. Ray put his arm around her shoulder and walked her into up the steps.

"Let's get you a cup of tea."

10

The meeting with Beatrice went surprisingly well, although she insisted on including candy-coated almonds at each place setting and placing them around the food area to bring good luck. That was easy enough.

But something still seemed off about what was going on. Who would cancel Autumn and Ray's wedding cake? Elizabeth gave the bakery a code-word to use, ensuring it was her, in case there were other changes. Someone surely meant to disrupt the wedding.

Elizabeth ordered the invitations online, triple checked them, added the dietary and guest responses to the RSVP cards, including who would bring their canine companion, and loaded the guest list into the app. Having them mailed directly from the printer removed the chance of anyone messing with them.

As pillars of the community, Autumn and Ray could have easily had five hundred guests, but they kept it to close family and friends: Autumn's neighbors, who essentially were her family after the death of her parents, Ray's parents, the Peabody Foundation board of directors, those who worked at the Peabody Mansion and Museum, and their latest friend, Dana Wood and her entourage, including the famous film director, Albert Holton. Everyone Autumn associated with loved her and felt loved in return. Elizabeth couldn't imagine who would want to upset her plans.

While Elizabeth wasn't superstitious, she researched bells to include in the ceremony, as Beatrice suggested. Elizabeth clicked the *submit* button on the order. Each guest would have a small bell to ring at the end of the ceremony and to keep as a remembrance of the day.

In the same order, she purchased a sweet little white wagon for Chrissy to ride in. Stephanie, Autumn's maid of honor, could pull it behind her carrying the rings. Elizabeth planned to decorate it with pink and white tulle wound around pink and white roses dipped in white glitter.

She would hold off ordering the food for the four-legged guests until she had a definite headcount. Pet parents could choose between a chicken or beef dish for their fur baby. Jodi Fallston, the chef, tested different recipes on the very-picky Chrissy, the slightly less picky Mickey, and on Ace, who would eat practically anything, and got it down to two of their favorites that they all agreed on.

Deciding where to have the fur babies eat was another story. It was a toss-up between keeping them near their pet parents at the tables or over to the side where all the pups could gather. She tried picturing Chrissy eating away from Autumn and couldn't, so decided to keep them with their pet parents until dessert. At that point, pet parents could select from a variety of natural handmade dog cookies and jerky treats, including grain-free. Bowls of water placed along the wall and cordoned off would prevent spillage from guests accidentally kicking them.

This was Elizabeth's first wedding project that included dogs. She'd add it to her portfolio for sure.

❄ ❄ ❄

Chrissy, Autumn, and her future mother-in-law, Carol Reed, took a ride to Center City, Philadelphia, to pick up the gowns and accessories. Megan greeted them and Autumn made introductions. Megan went to the back to get the order. When she returned ten minutes later, she held all but Autumn's wedding gown.

"I'm so sorry," said Megan.

"What do you mean?" asked Autumn.

She paused. "Your gown is missing."

"This is unacceptable!" Carol exclaimed.

Autumn appreciated having someone there to back her up. She'd been alone when the problem with the invitations occurred.

"It's not in the back, and I called the cleaner, but he doesn't have it."

"First it was the printer's fault, now it's the cleaner," Autumn mumbled.

"I want to talk to him right now," said Carol Reed.

"I can't just..." Megan said.

"You can either get him on the phone, give me his number, or his address. Your choice."

Autumn found a seat and plopped down, hugging Chrissy to stay calm. She didn't have the strength to fight.

Megan wrote the number and handed it to Carol, who snatched it from her hand.

"I'm really sorry," said Megan.

"That doesn't help us, now does it?" said Carol.

"You only have to pay for the items we do have while we continue to search for the wedding gown," Megan assured Autumn.

Autumn reached into her purse for her checkbook before Carol held out her hand and stopped her.

"You have to be kidding. We're not paying for anything until you find that wedding gown." Carol was resolute.

"But they're already altered. And Chrissy's accessory is custom made. I can't resell them!"

Carol glared at her. "And that wedding gown was one-of-a-kind. An antique. A family heirloom!"

All Megan could do was nod and stare at the floor while Carol dialed the cleaner on her cell phone.

"Hello, I'm calling for the status on an antique wedding gown dropped off for cleaning earlier in the week. It's under the name Autumn Clarke."

Autumn heard the name and thought this may be one of the last times anyone referred to her maiden name. No matter what went on with the gown, she planned to marry Ray, even if she wore jeans and a sweater. Well, a really nice sweater. Maybe cashmere.

Carol responded to the voice at the other end of the line.

"Well, where else could it be? Uh, huh. Uh, huh. I suggest you do another search on your premises and go through your security video to find it. Please keep the footage from the day the gown went missing. What is your address? Okay. Thank you."

Carol disconnected the call and sat next to Autumn and patted her hand.

"Don't worry, dear. We'll get it back."

Chrissy barked in agreement.

"That's right, Chrissy!" said Carol, petting her head.

Autumn looked at them with tears in her eyes.

They walked back to the car in stunned silence.

❄ ❄ ❄

"Ray, it was awful. Poor Autumn. She looked so hurt," Carol said.

"And shaken up. It's just another problem that makes Bea think there's a curse on the wedding. I don't want Autumn to believe it, too. That's why I left Ace with her. He makes her feel secure. Hopefully, they'll have something on the video footage."

"They promised me they'd hold on to it until I got there."

"You would've made a great cop, Mom." Ray smiled at her fortitude. Growing up, he'd relied on his mother to make sure the truth came out and justice was served. The day his bicycle went missing, Mom called everyone she knew on the street and then knocked on doors to see if one of the neighborhood kids took it. She found it within hours. Turned out, Timmy Nolan, the neighborhood bully, felt entitled to Ray's bike. Carol knew his mother from serving on a school committee together. Carol and Ray went to the Nolan's house to retrieve the bike and talk about the situation with Timmy and his parents. He got his bike, a new friend in Timmy, and Carol made an ally for her committee goals. Ray learned that day how persuasive his mother could be. He often thought she should've pursued a career in politics or law enforcement. Carol's determination to solve the wedding gown fiasco made Ray glad she was on his side.

They entered the cleaner's and Carol gave her name, then asked for the owner. He emerged from the back holding a compact disc.

"Here you are, Mrs. Reed. We found footage from the day the gown went missing. Looks like someone came through the back door during regular business hours. I can't explain how we didn't notice her."

"Did you report the theft to the police?" asked Ray.

"Yes, we filed a report with them and also with our insurance company. We'll reimburse you for the missing item."

"That's quite impossible," said Carol, "It's irreplaceable."

"May we have a tour of the area where the gown was stolen?" asked Ray, putting on his professional law enforcement voice, polite yet authoritative.

"This way."

The owner took them in the back and showed Ray and Carol where the work on specialty items took place.

"It was hanging here waiting for the final steaming to remove the wrinkles." He pointed to an empty rack with a single hook. Other gowns hung on a long rack, waiting for attention.

"Was anything else taken?" asked Ray.

"Not that we've noticed and no customers have inquired about missing garments."

Ray nodded.

"If we get it back, we'll be in touch. I'm very sorry for this situation."

"The gown belongs to my bride-to-be, and I appreciate anything you can do to get it back," said Ray, handing the man his card.

The shock on the man's face at seeing that Ray was a police lieutenant ensured he would do everything he could to rectify the situation.

"Of course," said the owner.

Ray took his mother's elbow and guided her out of the shop.

"Let's get this to Autumn's," he said. "We can watch it together."

❆ ❆ ❆

Ray and his mother let themselves in to his future home. They found Autumn sitting in front of the fire with Steve Coleman and Mickey, Ace and Chrissy all giving moral support. Steve brought some chocolate chip cookies from his daughter Lisa. They sat untouched on the coffee table.

"We got the video!" announced Carol.

Ray walked over to Autumn's laptop sitting on the ottoman and popped the disc into the machine. He brought it to the coffee table and slid the cookies to the side so they could all watch it together. He snatched a cookie for good measure.

For the first five minutes, nothing happened, but then a sliver of light came from the steel back door of the cleaning facility. A shadowy figure entered, looked around, and then headed to the left of the frame.

"That's the direction of the work area," said Ray. "Seems like the intruder knows the layout."

"It's hard to make out the face," said Carol. "The silhouette looks like a female given the shape of the body."

"And the hair," said Autumn. "It looks like a bun."

"She's also wearing high heels," said Steve, pointing to the screen.

"The person reminds me of Brittany, the woman who owns the shop where I ordered the invitations," said Autumn.

"But how would she know your gown was at the cleaner's?" asked Steve.

"Good question," said Ray.

"And why would she want to steal my wedding gown?"

"Another good question that begs an answer," said Ray.

"I say we bring Chrissy over to her shop to see if the gown is there. She'd sniffed the gown before Megan took it away," said Autumn.

She turned and put her forehead against Chrissy's. Autumn envisioned the gown hanging on the rack and Chrissy smelling it, then pushed the image toward Chrissy. Early on, Chrissy had revealed a special way of communicating that proved useful in solving crimes. The telepathic method usually worked with Chrissy, sending images to Autumn. This time, Autumn hoped it worked both ways. Autumn only used it for emergencies. She figured it was a divinely-ordained gift, not to be abused. The only other person who knew about this gift was Ray. Chrissy sent back a picture of the bottom of the gown. The images always came from Chrissy's perspective, much closer to the floor. It made Autumn dizzy.

"I'll go with you," said Carol. "Besides, I'd like to meet the incompetent person who messed up your invitation."

"Brittany said it was the printer's fault."

"Well, if she stole your gown, I suspect she had more to do with it than she says." Carol folded her arms, steadfast in her resolve to get justice for her daughter-in-law-to-be.

❄ ❄ ❄

Autumn, Chrissy, and Carol marched through the door of *Tying the Knot* wedding accessories shop. Brittany sat in her usual spot behind the desk.

"I'm surprised to see you," said Brittany, filing her nails.

"This is my soon-to-be mother-in-law, Carol," said Autumn.

"How are you?" responded Brittany.

Carol looked her up and down.

"I'm perplexed at how you showed up on a security video making off with Autumn's wedding gown."

"I don't know what you're talking about," said Brittany, putting down the nail file and looking at some papers on her desk.

Autumn finished wiping Chrissy's feet and let her off the leash.

"You don't mind, do you?" said Autumn.

"Chrissy is welcome to explore."

Autumn put her head against Chrissy's, giving her a picture of the wedding gown. Chrissy sniffed around the retail area and then followed the scent to the backroom.

Carol squinted at Brittany.

"I want the name of the printer who you claim ruined Autumn and Ray's invitations."

"Sorry, that's classified. I don't give away trade secrets."

"If my invitations are any indication, he'll put you out of business."

"I'm doing quite well, thanks."

Autumn looked around at the empty store. The same items she'd seen on her last visit were still there, dust surrounding them.

Chrissy let out a single bark. To Autumn, it sounded like *Mommy!* Autumn started toward the doorway to the employee area.

"Where do you think you're going?" Brittany said, rising from her chair.

"To get my baby." Autumn continued walking toward the door.

"You're not allowed back there!"

Brittany moved toward Autumn, and Carol stood in her way.

"Afraid of what we might find?"

Autumn hurried to the backroom. Chrissy barked again. She followed her fur baby's voice to a partially opened closet in the storage room and saw the hem of her wedding gown showing between the doorframe and the closet door. Throwing open the door, she saw the gown hung, uncovered but unharmed. She grabbed it and Chrissy and made her way to the front of the store. Autumn held it up in triumph and kissed Chrissy's cheek while Carol dialed Ray.

"Theft is a crime, missy," Carol said.

As Ray picked up, Brittany faked to the left, then ran around Carol and toward the front door.

"Stop!" Carol yelled, but Brittany was already out the door.

Autumn heard Ray on Carol's speaker. "What's going on there?"

Carol trotted after Brittany to see which direction she ran. Outside, the sidewalk was clear, with not even a passerby to question.

Winded, Carol said, "We found the gown. Rather, Chrissy found it. It was in the backroom of *Tying the Knot* in New Hope. The thief ran out the door. No coat. Wearing a tight, black pants outfit and red high-heeled pumps."

"Don't go chasing her, Mom!"

"I agree, Mom," Autumn said, trying out her new name for Carol. It was a little awkward at first, but was something she was happy to get used to.

"Is everyone okay?"

Autumn said, "We're fine. I'm glad to have my gown back."

Chrissy's tail wagged, and she licked her mommy's cheek.

"I'll contact William Moore to look for the owner. Brittany Farmer, correct?"

"Yes. And we'll call the cleaner to let him know we found the gown."

"I'll do that. I need to know if he wants to press charges. I'm assuming we do."

Autumn hesitated. She got the gown back, so did she want to make things worse?

Carol watched her. "Autumn, this person is out to get you for some reason."

"How do we know that? Maybe she's just having a rough time in her life."

"Your fiancé is too naïve, Ray. Talk some sense into her, will you?"

"We'll talk about it later. For now, let me call Moore to find Brittany. Autumn, I'll see you at your house." He hung up.

"Our house," she whispered.

"Let's find some plastic to protect your gown and get you and Chrissy home."

Autumn nodded.

Ace greeted them when they arrived at Autumn's house. She felt safe with him there. He had saved her from harm in the past, and she trusted his instincts.

Autumn ruffled the hair on his head. "You're such a good boy! Want a cookie?"

Ace wagged his tail and followed Autumn into the kitchen. Chrissy was close behind to consider the offerings at hand. Autumn handed Ace a large crunchy cookie, which he took and chomped it down. Chrissy turned her nose up and waited for something else. She also rejected a jerky snack, which Ace gobbled down without hesitation. Chrissy opted for a drink of water, which she delicately lapped from her crystal bowl.

Carol had the gown in hand. "Where do you want this?"

"Upstairs in the yellow guest room at the top of the stairs, please. Either on the back of the door or in the closet."

Carol took care of it and came back down.

"Want to call Mr. Reed, er, uh, Pop, and see if he wants to come over for dinner?"

Carol smiled. "Sure, dear. I'm sure he'd love to."

Autumn would get the hang of calling them Mom and Pop. It would just take a little time.

A knock on the door sent Chrissy and Ace barking. Autumn looked out of the peephole.

"Stephanie!"

Her best friend took Autumn in her arms and held her.

"I heard what happened! Are you alright?"

Autumn pulled away. "Where did you hear?"

"Adam. Ray told him, so he called me to make sure you were okay."

Leave it to Adam to relay important information to Stephanie. Autumn took Stephanie's coat and hung it in the entryway closet.

"Thanks for checking on me. Come in. Ray's mom is here."

They joined her in the den.

"Hi, Stephanie. Nice to see you, dear."

"You, as well. So, you were there when this all happened?"

"There? She chased Brittany out the door!" Autumn could smile at it now that they were home.

"Ran out without a coat. And how can you run on icy sidewalks in high heels?"

"Wouldn't be easy, that's for sure. Maybe it'll help the police catch her faster."

"Ray's dad is coming for dinner. Want to stay? You can call Adam to join us, if he's free."

"Sounds great! Are we starting with wine?"

"I can get that. Red or white?" Carol went to the wine rack in the kitchen.

Autumn liked how comfortable Carol was in the house.

"I'll start dinner," said Autumn.

"No, you won't! Let's order out," Carol insisted.

Exhausted after the day she'd had, Autumn didn't have to be convinced.

"What are you in the mood for?"

"How about Thai food?" Stephanie suggested.

"We love Thai cuisine," said Carol.

Autumn dug a menu, pad, and pen out of the kitchen junk drawer and handed it to Carol, who wrote their choices and handed everything to Stephanie.

Autumn called for delivery while Carol poured the wine. She opened one bottle of each to go with the various food choices.

"To all things going right from now on!" Stephanie toasted.

"I'm all for that," said Autumn.

They clinked glasses.

While they waited for their men and the delivery person to arrive, Autumn fixed dinner for Chrissy and Ace.

"My special little girl. What would I do without you?" she cooed while filling Chrissy's bowl with fresh meat and vegetables. Chrissy's doctor suggestion was a brand that was more like human food and formulated with the help of veterinarians. Chrissy loved it, which said a lot. She was the pickiest pup around.

Ace liked it, too, but he liked anything. He just ate triple the amount Chrissy got, given his size. Ace dove in and devoured his portion, while Chrissy took a dainty mouthful and chewed her food thoroughly. She looked up at her mommy with loving eyes.

"I love you, too, sweetheart," said Autumn, and went to join the others in the den.

Their dinner finished, the pups ran to Autumn and then to the sliding door. She grabbed Chrissy's coat and secured the Velcro straps before opening the door. They both charged across the patio and into the snow. Chrissy started in the shoveled area and then ventured into deeper drifts until the snow trapped her.

Ace tried pushing her forward, but Autumn had to run out and get her. Cradling her fur baby, Autumn ran into the house, removed Chrissy's coat, and grabbed a warm cloth. She recruited Stephanie to get one for Ace to remove the snowballs from his long hair.

Carol surprised them by building a roaring fire for them to cozy up to.

Ray, his dad, Kevin, and Adam arrived within minutes of each other and right before the food delivery person pulled up.

They washed up while Autumn and Stephanie unpacked the food. Carol brought them glasses of wine. They sat around the dining room table, Ace at Ray's feet and Chrissy near Autumn.

Having everyone here made Autumn feel safe. She picked at her food. Some people eat when they're stressed. Autumn was the opposite.

"Did they find Brittany?" Autumn asked.

"Not yet," said Ray, swallowing a forkful of Pad Thai. "William Moore said he'd call as soon as he knew anything."

"Was the gown damaged?" asked Adam, taking a sip of red wine.

"Thankfully, no," said Carol. "What I don't understand is Brittany's motive."

"We got a warrant and searched the shop for any clues. We also found and searched her apartment. Handwritten notes look similar to the lettering on the box of knives. My guess is she sent those, too," said Ray.

"We found the name of the printer she uses," Adam said between bites of Mussaman Curry. "He told us he printed the invitations exactly as Brittany instructed."

"No one at her apartment complex has seen her today. We have an APB out on her vehicle." Ray said.

"I don't even know this woman except to do business with her. What does she have against me?"

"Jealousy?" Stephanie offered. "You're loved and inherited a fortune. Love and money. Two things she probably wants desperately."

"I saw a crime show that said those are the two most frequent motives for murder," said Kevin, forking a chunk of pecan-encrusted salmon into his mouth.

"That's probably true," said Ray, "but people can have actual or delusional reasons for wanting to harm someone. We can't be sure of her motives, at least until I can question her."

"Why would she run from a theft, regardless of the motive? The penalty can't be that severe," said Carol.

"What if she's involved in that recent murder?" Kevin asked. "Her shop is down the street from where Chrissy found Angela Curry's body."

Ray put down his fork and stared at his father.

"You know, Pop, that's something to consider."

≉11≉

Pamela Brown got the word that Brittany Farmer had stolen Autumn Clarke's wedding gown and immediately began researching Brittany's background. She found Brittany opened her shop a couple of years ago. Searches of her identification showed that her Pennsylvania driver's license issued around the same time she opened *Tying the Knot*.

Expanding the search parameters got her at least twenty-five women named Brittany Farmer.

With Brittany still on the loose, Pamela couldn't interview her directly, so she relied on William Moore for information. With two open cases, the murder of Angela Curry and the fugitive thief, Brittany Farmer, Moore had to come up with something for her show, but information was slow in coming.

From time to time, Detective Moore got a case of morality and clammed up. But Pamela knew how to open him up with a reminder that she knew about his crush on Autumn. It was easy to throw suspicion on him for sabotaging the wedding with that tidbit of information. She liked to use speculation during her podcast and could imply with no proof that he and Brittany worked together to undermine Autumn and Ray's wedding plans. Tantalizing her audience gave her a rush and made them tune in for every broadcast.

She'd speak to Brittany directly on air, asking her to dial-in and talk to listeners, and tell her side of the story.

❀ ❀ ❀

Terri Cromwell organized her notes for the Reed wedding. The encounter with Barry during her meeting with Autumn horrified her; his lack of decorum offensive. Now, as so many times before, she needed to make up for it.

Thankfully, Barry's temporary visit would end before the wedding, and he could go back to the facility in the Pocono Mountains, where they give him the care he needed. When he was here, his behavior worsened. Maybe it was from memories of his father and the resentment he had after he'd left them.

At least when Angela Curry was alive, Barry could have a session with her to calm down. After meeting with Angela, Barry was better for a couple of days or so. But without her, he had no one to talk to when he was here. She was the only one he spoke highly of and mostly behaved around. He thanked her for recommending the group home in the mountains, saying he enjoyed being in nature and around others similar to him.

Angela shared with Terri that her son had deep delusions about himself, his level of intelligence, and his effect on others. Barry fancied himself as someone of high intellect, looking down upon others as if they lacked sense. He misconstrued information and made it fit into his fantasy world of deception and conspiracies. Any challenge to these delusions set him off, so Terri let Angela manage him when he was home.

After the news of Angela Curry's death, Barry changed back to his angry, obnoxious self and hadn't been right since. Terri Cromwell considered an earlier return to the Poconos for her son so he could return to his self-protected bubble of delusion and monitored medications.

❄ ❄ ❄

Autumn's caller ID showed an incoming call from Megan Harris. She answered with misgiving.

"Thank goodness you found the gown!" said Megan.

Autumn paced up and back in the kitchen, thinking before responding.

"Yes, we're quite relieved."

A heavy pause came between them.

"When will you pick up your order? The wedding is next week, isn't it?"

Autumn took a deep breath. Chrissy pawed her leg, pulling her from her thoughts. She was ready to scrap the formality of the wedding plans and have an intimate ceremony with immediate family. But to be fair, Megan had the other gowns altered and the beading on her dress secured. Compensating her for that was the right thing to do.

Her thoughts took up more time than she realized, when Megan said, "How about I have everything delivered to save you a trip into town?"

Autumn hesitated. How had Brittany known where her gown was? Megan was the only one who knew where its location.

Autumn didn't even know which cleaner until her mom-to-be demanded the information. Carol was really something. Autumn's internal lie detector was on full blast when it came to Megan.

After the odd delivery of knives to the Peabody Mansion, she was reluctant to give out her home address. She gave the address of the bed-and-breakfast and disconnected the call, hoping this was the last interaction she'd have with Megan. She could always have Carol and Beatrice greet her instead.

She lifted Chrissy and kissed her ear. Chrissy pressed against her mommy.

"It's good to have people in our corner, isn't it, sweetheart?"

The white sedan pulled up at the Peabody Mansion B&B. Ward stood at the entrance to the woodland trail, his figure as imposing as the *Foo Dogs* he stood between, watching the woman sporting a tight bun, winter white suit, and cream-colored, fur-collared coat open her door and carefully touch down with a heeled shoe on the paved driveway. The driveway was clear of snow, yet she walked as though it was coated with a sheet of ice . He walked over to the car and waited for her to notice him.

"Oh!" said Megan, jumping back. "I didn't see you there, but now that you're here, I could use some help."

Ward crossed his arms. "With what?"

She opened the back door and pulled out hangers tied together and covered in long opaque plastic with the words *With This Ring*, Philadelphia, PA imprinted on them.

"You're the woman who lost Autumn's wedding gown," said Ward, sneering at her.

Megan looked at the ground as she handed him the gowns.

Ward took them and headed toward the front door. Beatrice and Carol stood like sentinels watching Megan dig for the veil and other purchases.

She shut the car door and proceeded to the front door, stopping halfway when she saw Carol. Beatrice stood next to Carol, scowling, a check in her hand.

Carol took the gowns from Ward and put them in the study. He stayed put next to Beatrice.

Megan pasted on a counterfeit smile. *Just like the rest of her,* thought Ward.

"Here's the rest. Chrissy's headpiece, Autumn's veil, and the blue garter."

When no one reached out to take them, she stretched her arms toward them. Carol returned and silently took the bags from Megan.

"I don't know why you're all mad at me! I didn't steal the gown!"

"You were the only one who knew where it was. I'll bet you told Brittany. She wouldn't have known otherwise!" said Carol accusingly.

Ward smiled inwardly. He liked Carol's spunk.

Cornered, Megan admitted, "Yes, well, I did call Brittany to tell her how beautiful the gown was, but how was I to know she'd steal it?"

"You told her more than that, missy!" said Beatrice, glowering at Megan. "What business of hers is the cleaner taking care of Autumn's gown?"

"Well, I..."

"Here's your check. I tried talking Autumn out of paying you, but she said it wouldn't be right. Take it and go," Beatrice said, dismissing Megan.

Ward liked the protective way Beatrice spoke about Autumn.

"Any idea where Brittany is now?" Ward asked.

"No, uh, no idea, I, we're not that close."

"C'mon now," said Carol. "If that's true, you would've called someone else to sing the praises of the wedding gown."

"Right! And I heard Autumn tell you what happened with the invitations," said Beatrice, jabbing a finger in Megan's direction. "That makes it even worse that you called Brittany about the gown."

"I, I..."

"Just go," said Carol. "I heard Pamela Brown's podcast, and she's outing you and Brittany every chance she gets."

"Won't be good for business, I'll tell you that," said Ward with a smirk.

Megan made a guttural sound that reminded Ward of a severe allergy sufferer choking for breath. The three filled the doorway, their energy pushing Megan down the front steps and toward her car. She didn't look back, got in the car, slammed the door shut, and peeled out of the driveway.

"Good riddance," said Beatrice.

The others nodded their agreement.

"Is it true that Pamela Brown is talking about her on the podcast?" asked Beatrice.

"No. Not yet, anyway. I plan to make an anonymous call to Ms. Brown telling her all about it," said Carol. "No one messes with my daughter-to-be."

Ward chuckled. "I'm glad we're on the same side, Carol."

Beatrice smiled slyly. "We make a formidable team!"

⸗12⸗

Autumn, Ray, and the pups snuggled on the couch, exhausted from the latest craziness around the wedding. She considered a larger sofa to give the four of them more room.

"We could have eloped, you know," said Autumn, stroking Chrissy's silky hair.

"And disappoint my mother? Not a chance."

"I love your mother. She said I can call her 'Mom'."

"You're the only one she's ever given that privilege to."

"What about Patty? Weren't you engaged?"

"No. We lived together, but I never said I'd marry her."

He looked at Autumn.

"I was waiting for you."

"Then you're lucky I showed up," Autumn laughed.

"I am," Ray said and squeezed her shoulder.

"Well, since we're going through with the wedding, I need to know if it's okay to let Harry Halifax work on our ice sculpture."

"He's still a suspect."

"Can you clear him faster? Elizabeth is having trouble getting another sculptor."

"Worst-case scenario, we don't have an ice sculpture."

Ace shifted on the couch, stretching and baring his tummy to Ray for scratching, his large paw dangling in Chrissy's face. Everyone moved to accommodate him. Ray rubbed Ace in the spot that made his leg pound the air. Chrissy sneezed at Ace's appendage and went onto Autumn's lap. Ace lifted his head and looked at her, seeming to say. *What did I do?*

Yes, a much bigger couch, thought Autumn.

"We confiscated the tools that are the shape of the chest wound to see if there's blood on them. Faith Halifax cleaned all the tools in his shop and truck, so it's going to take longer than I'd like to get the lab results back."

"Why would she do that?"

"Seems it's her normal routine at the end of his workday."

"Do you think Brittany fits into this mess as your dad suggested?"

"He wants you to call him 'Pop,' so get used to saying it."

Autumn blushed and nodded.

"I've been thinking about that. What's the motive? Yes, she likely had the opportunity. But the wound. She doesn't have tools shaped like that."

"What if Harry's truck was on the street unlocked while he had his session with Angela?"

"That's a good thought. I'll question Harry again to see if that's a possibility."

❋ ❋ ❋

Ray called Harry Halifax down to his office at the Knollwood police station for questioning. It was more private than dealing with Detective William Moore at the New Hope station or at home, where his wife lurked around. Moore had been slow in providing information to Ray. His questions about Autumn every time they met for police business made Ray suspect it was more than polite conversation. He caught him looking at Autumn when she was nearby with desire in his eyes.

Ray wasn't the jealous type, but he was highly protective, especially of Autumn. The vibe William Moore gave off made Ray suspect he resented his pending marriage. He didn't mention it to Autumn, and it was too late to take him off the guest list, but Ray watched interactions between Autumn and Moore vigilantly.

Autumn had a habit of talking to anyone, her friendly demeanor attracting many. She wouldn't think that a person might have selfish motives toward her. That's what Ray and Ace were there for. Now he could also rely on his mother's fierce protection. His mother had a strong sense of danger and was ready to thwart any threat. He was more like her than his father.

With Harry Halifax's wife, Faith, it might be the same with her protecting her husband, at all costs.

Ray saw Harry stroll into the station, relaxed and smiling. Ace spotted him and barked once.

"Hey there, fella," said Harry, reaching out his palm toward Ace to sniff, then sat down at the chair across from Ray.

"Thanks for coming in, Harry."

"Sure, no problem." He sat back and crossed his leg.

"Tell me about your relationship with Angela Curry."

Harry looked at the ceiling, lost in memory for a moment.

"Ah, Angela. She was something."

"How so?" Ray sat back, mimicking Harry's posture. Ace stayed in erect guard dog position.

"It started as a professional interaction. I was in a deep depression. It affected my work. There was no spark, no joy. I heard about Dr. Curry from a friend."

Ray had his notebook in his lap. He scribbled as Harry spoke.

"Who's the friend?"

"William Moore. He said Angela helped him a while back."

No wonder Moore was dragging his feet in this case.

"When did Detective Moore question you about the night Dr. Curry died?"

"He hasn't called me, unless he left a message and I didn't get it."

Ray noted Moore hadn't followed-up on a likely suspect.

"Did it help to speak with Dr. Curry?"

"The results surprised me. I emerged from the funk and saw her in a way I didn't intend to. She made advances, and I didn't say no." Harry folded his hands in his lap.

"Did your wife know?"

"I didn't even tell her I was getting therapy, let alone sleeping with Angela."

"I understand you were her last patient the night she of the murder."

Harry shifted in his chair.

"Now wait a minute. If you're accusing me of killing her, you're way off base."

Ray leaned forward, elbows on his desk.

"Harry, you were at her office the night she died," Ray said forcefully. Ace stood. Ray petted him to let him know to stay.

"True, but I would never hurt her. She was alive when I left."

Ray felt like he'd hit a wall so tried a different tack.

"Where was your vehicle parked?"

"Across the street from her office."

"Was it locked?"

"Probably. I usually lock the doors. I have expensive tools in the back. They're costly to replace."

"So, you locked the back door."

"I believe so. I came right from a job. I put my tools back there and shut the door." He thought for a few beats. "It's possible I locked the driver and passenger doors, but not the back door. I'm honestly not sure."

Ray made a note.

"What do you think happened to Dr. Curry?"

Ace moved closer to Harry, staring him down. Ray didn't stop him this time. His suspect was holding back. Maybe Ace could jar his confession loose. Harry slid the chair back a little.

"I don't have the foggiest idea. I was just trying to get away from her."

A bead of sweat trickled down Harry's temple. He brushed it away and wiped his hand on his jeans.

"Tell me what happened before you left Dr. Curry's office."

Harry glanced at Ace, who held his gaze.

"Well, I, uh, she, uh, we…"

"Just breathe and tell me what you remember."

Harry took a few breaths and rubbed his hands across his pants.

"We argued."

"About what?"

"She wanted me to leave my wife! If I didn't, she was going to tell Faith about the affair."

"How did that make you feel?"

"Horrified! Listen, I've been with many women, but they mean nothing to me. My wife is everything!"

Ray tried not to judge, but if his wife meant the world to him, why cheat? He couldn't see being with anyone but Autumn.

"And then what happened?"

"I told her I never planned to leave Faith. She accused me of using her."

"And then?"

"There was nothing left for me to do but leave. I couldn't control what she'd do next. I had to get away from her. Got in my truck and took off."

"Did you tell Faith about the indiscretion?"

"Didn't have to. I heard about Angela's murder that day. I'll be honest, I felt relieved."

Ray nodded.

"I'll have to question Mrs. Halifax."

"Do you have to tell her about the affair?"

"It would give her motive."

Harry looked at his wringing hands.

"We have to find out who killed Angela, so whatever you need to do, Lieutenant Reed."

Ray nodded.

"Was there anyone on the street when you left?"

"It was dark, around nine o'clock. The street was empty and quiet as far as I could tell."

"Any idea who would have a grudge against her?"

"It could be so many people. She knew everything about everybody. She actually said that people in this area should be careful about crossing her."

Ray jotted down the threat and then snapped his fingers. Ace went behind Ray's desk and sat next to him.

"Thanks for your cooperation, Mr. Halifax. I appreciate you coming in. If you think of anything else, please call me directly." Ray handed him a card.

Alone with Ace, he petted his friend's head. "You're such a good boy. Way to intimidate Harry. Do you think he did it?"

Ace was the best lie detector Ray ever saw. Ace stared at Ray. He took that as a no.

Ray dialed Autumn and gave her permission to have Harry Halifax make the ice sculpture. The wedding was getting close and there was no time to waste.

Then he called William Moore, who picked up on the first ring.

"Hey, Ray. How's it going?"

"Fine. There's new information about the case. How about we meet up and share what we have so far?"

After a brief hesitation, Detective Moore agreed to meet Ray at Lisa Coleman's café.

Ray sat with a cup of hot cocoa that Lisa insisted he have, given the frigid weather, when Moore showed up.

"That smells good," he said with an uncharacteristic toothy smile. "I'll have one of those, too," Moore told the server.

Ray was glad to see Lisa having help in her business. She stretched herself too thin. But she liked to wait on special customers herself, and she showed up next to his table.

"Hi guys," she said. "Staying for lunch?"

"I could go for the chicken Florentine sandwich," Ray said.

"What's on it?" asked William.

"Chicken breast, spinach, tomatoes, and provolone cheese."

"Sounds good."

Lisa walked away and came back with two cups of her minestrone soup. She placed them on the table with crackers.

"Perfect for a snowy day. On the house."

Lisa walked away before Ray could argue about paying for it.

William took a spoonful. "Wow, that's good. I need to come here more often."

The server came back with William's hot cocoa and two glasses of water.

"How's that lovely lady of yours?"

"Autumn is fine. Focusing on wedding details."

"Tell her I said hello. She's a real catch."

"Don't I know it?" Ray said, wanting to change the subject. "So, how's the case coming along? Any updates?" He wiped his mouth.

"I checked with the pathologist, but they haven't identified the type of weapon used. They said there was very little blood. Probably happened around nine the evening before." He crumbled a two-pack of crackers into his soup.

Ray already knew that, but didn't let on.

"Any news on the whereabouts of Brittany Farmer?"

"She seems to have disappeared off the face of the earth. No one has seen her around her apartment or her shop. What she did to Autumn was awful. Tell Autumn I'll get her no matter what."

Wanting to be Autumn's hero, Ray thought.

"Have you spoken with Harry Halifax?"

Detective Moore's spoon stopped for a quick moment on the way to his mouth.

"No, I haven't."

"He was the last client Dr. Curry saw before being killed."

"How did you find that out?"

"The attorney closing out her office."

"What's happening to Angela's files?"

Interesting that Moore used her familiar name rather than a formal reference and didn't mention Harry Halifax.

"Being transferred to new psychologists in the area. It's in the best interest of her clients."

Detective Moore kept his eyes on the soup rather than meeting Ray's gaze.

"What do you make of Harry being there that night?" Moore asked, moving his empty soup cup to the table's edge.

"Ice sculptors use a tool shaped like the wound in Dr. Curry's chest. I questioned him."

William Moore released the breath he was holding.

"Harry is a good suspect, then."

"We'll see."

Ray didn't want to reveal he'd already eliminated him from the suspect pool.

"Seems obvious, doesn't it? His tool, last one on the scene."

"Mr. Halifax told me Dr. Curry threatened her clients with what she knew about them. That substantially widens the suspect pool."

"Did he say what she knew?" said Moore, jaw tight.

"No, but she worked with the New Hope Police Department for officers with PTSD, didn't she?"

"Yeah, I remember her working with some officers."

"Did you ever work with her? You had a shooting incident last year that was pretty traumatic."

"The department required me to have a few sessions. It didn't seem to help, so once I satisfied the requirement, I stopped going."

Ray paused, sipping his hot chocolate, to see if Moore would open up a bit more.

"What else did he say, Ray?"

"You referred him to Dr. Curry."

The server set down their sandwiches and left when they said they needed nothing else right now.

"How well do you know Harry Halifax, William?"

"Not well."

"It's still a conflict of interest for you to be on a case where he's a suspect. Tell you what, I'll deal with the murder investigation. You focus on finding Farmer."

"It's best if I'm kept in the loop. The Chief may not like it."

"I can talk to him for you."

Moore gave a humorless chuckle. "Just as well. I've been so busy looking for Brittany Farmer, I guess this case got away from me."

Ray doubted that.

Moore focused on his sandwich and talked about the weather and icy road conditions as he watched the new snowfall dusting the streets.

≠13≠

Chrissy charged to the door, wagging her tail. From the reaction, Autumn knew that Steve Coleman and Mickey were here to visit. Mickey's ears were cold on the outer layer of hair, but warm nearer his skin when she petted him.

"Want to go for a walk with us?" Steve asked, wiping his feet.

"Not right now. I'm going through the RSVPs and jotting down who wants to eat what, who's bringing a fur baby or a plus one, and doing the seating chart."

"Can we help?"

"Come into the kitchen. Chrissy could use some fun time with Mickey and you could use something to warm you up."

Autumn had a pot of lentil soup simmering on the stove.

The pups ran into the den to Chrissy's toy pile. Of all the friends Chrissy had, Mickey was her favorite. She enjoyed having Ace around, but it was different with Mickey. He'd been her first friend when coming to live with Autumn. When the standard poodle was feeling under the weather a few months ago, Chrissy dragged Autumn down to his house and insisted on sitting with him. Autumn obliged, since the veterinarian confirmed it wasn't contagious. Chrissy's presence seemed to comfort Mickey. Autumn knew the feeling. The Shih Tzu had a soul that healed those in distress, both furry and human.

Ever since, Mickey had watched over Chrissy, as did Ace. If there was a dog nearby that Chrissy didn't like, she'd hide under Mickey, for her stature fit perfectly beneath his long legs, shielding her from harm. His elegant appearance belied his strong bark and protective nature.

She heard them bark near the sliding door.

"Okay, okay. Let's get your coat on, little one."

Autumn dressed Chrissy for the snow and opened the door so they could play outside. Mickey's white, curly hair camouflaged him, but his black nose and eyes made him visible.

A big mug of lentil soup steamed in front of Steve.

"Did you hear the latest from Pamela Brown's podcast?" he asked.

"What did she say?"

"That Angela Curry had dirt on everybody in the New Hope area, and Pamela Brown vowed to her audience that she'd bring it all to light."

"Where is she getting her information from?"

"She didn't say, but also mentioned that your wedding seemed to be back on for now."

"For now?" Autumn exclaimed. "Maybe the dry cleaner told her about the stolen wedding dress and that we got it back."

"It's possible," said Steve, "since she added that there's a hunt for Brittany Farmer and asked her to contact the show to tell her side."

Autumn put her head in her hand.

"Why is she so fascinated by our wedding, and why would anyone care?"

"Like it or not, you're a celebrity. People are curious."

Autumn shook her head and took a spoonful of lentils.

"I don't think we're that interesting. Just trying to live a normal life."

"There nothing usual about being an heiress and marrying a member of the police force."

"A better story would be about the local animal shelters and the fur babies who need forever homes."

"That isn't juicy enough for Pamela Brown's show. She wants gossip."

"I'll bet Ray could find out how Ms. Brown gets her information."

Steve's eyebrows went up, and he smiled knowingly.

The pups were at the door, barking to be let in. Autumn and Steve sprung into action to get them cleaned up and warm. Chrissy moaned with pleasure as Autumn snuggled her, dried her hair, and kissed her head.

"Let me know when you have time for a walk. We miss you."

"We miss you guys, too. Give me a couple of days."

"You got it."

❄ ❄ ❄

Barry Cromwell paced on the sidewalk outside the former office of Dr. Angela Curry. His heated breath sent steam pouring from his mouth. Fit to burst at the situation that led to Dr. Curry's demise, he was at a loss to get rid of the pent-up energy. How could this happen? Guilt overwhelmed him. It was all his fault.

He hit himself in the head, open-palmed.

He wanted to go back to the mountains where he was safe, but he wasn't due back for a couple more days. Being around his mother made him angry. She was the reason his father had left. It was shortly after Dr. Curry told them Barry needed a lot of care. She contacted a psychiatrist to get him medication. She said it would "even him out" so he had fewer outbursts. It was right after he'd attacked his mother. And then his father left.

He didn't want his mother taking him back to the mountains. Being in the car with her for almost two hours was more than he could stand. She'd go on and on about the wonderful visit, when he knew that wasn't true. She lied. He felt it. She didn't want him there, and she told everybody what a loser he was.

He went up to Dr. Curry's door and punched the sign that hung there. Blood oozed from scraped knuckles. It was Dr. Curry's fault that he was home this week.

Megan's heart sank as the last customers picked up their dresses. Calling the people with orders waiting to be picked up and arranging drop shipments for those remaining allowed her to close the shop for good. Collecting the money in full from all of them gave her a tidy sum with which to leave town.

Between that gossip-monger, Pamela Brown, talking about Brittany Farmer's theft and Autumn Clarke's entourage of bodyguards, Megan knew her business would die anyway if she stayed in Philadelphia.

She called Maureen Roberts, the realtor who'd sold Megan her cottage in the Poconos, to sell the building and her house in Ardmore. The savvy realtor promised the properties would sell in a jiffy, giving Megan enough money to go to the mountains and hide out for a while until she figured out her next move. It was after they signed contracts that Maureen mentioned she was a friend of Autumn Clarke. Megan hoped Maureen wouldn't share her plans with Autumn. It was too late to call another realtor, so whatever information she shared, Megan would deal with later.

If Angela Curry hadn't introduced her to Brittany Farmer, none of this would have happened. From the moment she'd met Dr. Curry, her anxiety and depression worsened. Weekly appointments an hour away in New Hope stressed her schedule. She made the most of it by going to dinner at one of the boutique restaurants in area. Dr. Curry knew about her bridal business and introduced her to Brittany Farmer at *Tying the Knot* to see if there was a way to support one another's businesses.

And everything went downhill from there.

Megan's business was fine before that. Her energy took a dip after her mother's death. Mom had helped at the shop, and it was never the same without her. That brought on grief and depression. She worked too many hours, further exhausting herself. A friend recommended she try Dr. Curry. Having tried everything else, Megan decided it couldn't hurt to see if therapy might make a difference.

Between Angela Curry and Brittany Farmer, she felt like she had more support than before. They understood her sense of loss and need for someone to lean on. Both took advantage. Brittany used her to get to Autumn's gown, and Dr. Curry threatened to reveal her one-night-stand with the groom of one of her customers.

Megan didn't want to pay for her indiscretion with her reputation, so she paid in favors to Dr. Curry. As directed, Megan shared the secrets and activities of her customers with whomever Angela Curry told her to, most often Brittany Farmer, Pamela Brown, and William Moore. For some reason, they were all interested in Autumn Clarke and Raymond Reed. Megan felt bad for betraying the couple. As far as she could tell, they had wronged no one.

Megan grew to hate both Brittany Farmer and Dr. Curry. With every breath she took, Megan knew that the world was better off without Dr. Angela Curry and felt no guilt over her demise.

She took one last look around the shop she loved and lost, locked the doors, and walked toward an unknown future.

14

Chrissy let out her Mickey's at-the-door bark. Steve stood there bundled up for the latest snowfall, and Mickey wagged his tail. Autumn threw on her heavy coat, scarf, and hat and dressed Chrissy in her pink quilted snow jacket, lined with fleece. She turned up the collar to keep her a little neck warm. A pink knit hat that tied under the chin completed the outfit. She didn't put the boots on, knowing she'd throw them off after a few steps. Autumn clicked the leash onto the metal ring of Chrissy's harness and pulled on her thickest gloves. When she was a child, her mother had always dressed Autumn in layers to play in the snow, and she adhered to that strategy to this day.

"Could we have picked a colder day?" she asked.

"It's brisk, sure, but the pups love it."

Autumn watched the friends trot down the snowy sidewalk side-by-side.

"Don't you think Mickey needs a coat?"

"He's never complained before."

Autumn considered Mickey as he walked, surefooted and comfortable, as though it were a spring day. The fancy hairdo, with longer puffs of hair on his head, ears, legs, and tail, complemented Mickey's trimmed torso, which Steve kept on the longer side during the winter months. The water-resistant curly hair looked dense and warm.

"Taking a walk is a pleasant break from the wedding stuff. It's so much work and not as much fun as I thought it would be."

"It's not just the usual wedding planning. You're dealing with a stolen wedding gown, a canceled wedding cake, messed up invitations, and Chrissy finding another body. You've had to do everything twice!"

"That puts a new spin on why I feel so spent." A blast of cold air had her pulling the thick scarf around her chin.

"On top of that, Pamela Brown blasting your strife on the airwaves adds even more stress."

"Thanks for the reminder."

"What can Mickey and I do to help? Reporting what I hear isn't enough."

"Knowing what's going on is important. I don't keep my finger on local goings-on the way I should."

Steve raised the zipper on his jacket, closing it all the way up.

"Has Ray narrowed down the suspect list?"

"He eliminated Harry Halifax from the list."

"I'd think he was the most obvious culprit having an affair and being the last to see Dr. Curry alive."

"True, but it's unlikely he'd use a tool specific to his work to commit the crime."

"Maybe it's what he had on hand."

"Harry claims it was in his truck. He wouldn't bring a tool into his session. Besides, Angela Curry threatened him at the end of their session. He'd have no reason to bring a murder weapon in with him."

"Especially if he expected lovemaking rather than an argument."

"Exactly."

Steve smiled. "At least you'll have the ice sculpture you wanted."

"Wait until you see it. Elizabeth made sure it would be the perfect one. I don't know what I'd do without her."

Autumn's cell phone rang. It was Maureen Roberts.

"Hi Autumn. Are you sure you and Ray don't want to move from your parents' house? I just listed a beautiful property in Ardmore."

"No, thanks. We're excited to stay where we are. Besides, he needs to be in Knollwood for work."

"Thought you'd reconsider when you found out it belongs to Megan Harris, your bridal consultant."

"Not after putting my gown in danger, she's not."

"Not to worry, she's moving out of the area to her cottage in the mountains. Closed the shop and everything. She won't have a chance to upset the applecart on any more weddings."

"Good to know," said Autumn, raising her eyebrows at Steve.

"What?" he whispered.

Autumn held up a finger.

"Did you get your invitation?"

"Absolutely! It's the most thorough RSVP card I've ever seen. I'll be coming solo and can't wait to mingle."

"We're looking forward to having you. See you soon, Maureen!"

"Toodle-oo!"

Autumn disconnected the call, mouth wide in shock, and ready to share the latest with Steve.

"I wonder what made Megan take such drastic action," he said.

"It was probably getting hit with both barrels from Bea and Carol, and a kick to the head by Ward when she dropped off my order. They waited for her at the mansion and let her have it."

Steve shook from the thought.

"Better Megan than me. I wouldn't want to be a target squirming in their sights!"

"Nor would I. I'm lucky they're on my side."

❋ ❋ ❋

As Autumn's best friend since college, Stephanie Douglas researched ideas for bachelorette parties. The entertainment Autumn enjoyed was not the usual stripper-drinking-acting-crazy kind. Stephanie had to get creative. One idea was a murder mystery dinner, but she couldn't bring Chrissy. Besides, Autumn solved murder mysteries in her normal life. There had to be something better.

If Autumn had waited until spring as originally planned, there would be more options, but the winter limited outdoor activities, unless they wanted to brave the weather.

A brilliant idea popped into her mind: a spa day with all the ladies at a five-star mountain resort that also had a fabulous restaurant. They could drive up in a stretch limo in the morning and get back by nine o'clock the same night. The ninety-minute drive was enough to have some fun in the limo, like breakfast and mimosas on the way up and wine on the way back.

Now to find someone to take care of Chrissy for the day. To get Autumn to relax might be impossible if she worried about Chrissy. They had been together since the day Autumn had adopted her.

A call to Ray should do the trick. If Ray and Ace watched Chrissy, Autumn could relax. Maybe invite Steve Coleman and Mickey for good measure. Stephanie would have dinner delivered to them, and everything would go smoothly.

A few phone calls later, Ray and Steve agreed to watch Chrissy so the women could celebrate Autumn's transition to her new life. Stephanie arranged a limo to fit herself, Autumn, Elizabeth Johnson, Kim Stokes, Carol Reed, Beatrice Peabody, Chef Sarah Kelly, Stacey Eldridge, Lisa Coleman, Judge Terri Cromwell, and

Autumn's neighbor, Julie Hall. She invited the famous actor, Dana Wood, as she and Autumn had become friends when she stayed at the mansion in October, but she was filming a movie that day and promised to make it to the wedding. Stacey was reluctant to leave her miniature poodle, Clay, home alone, so Ray suggested she leave Clay with them.

With Ace, Mickey, and Clay, Chrissy had a party of her own going on. Julie's Yorkshire terrier, Teddy, would stay with her husband, Brad, but Ray invited him to be with the men. He also invited Stephanie's boyfriend and Ray's best man, Adam Miller, to join the men's gathering. She clapped her hands and smiled at how perfectly her plan fell into place.

"Ray is like Autumn in that he doesn't want any crazy bachelor party," Adam said to Stephanie. "I'll invite a few more guys and make it a proper party for him. I'll order the food and drinks."

"Don't forget food for the canine guests!" Stephanie reminded him. "And Jasper Wiggins, Beatrice's housemate, would probably appreciate an invitation, since Beatrice will be with us."

"What's the story with those two? Are they, you know, together?"

"He's her house manager, and they've grown closer these past months. Ever since the Halloween Extravaganza, he looks smitten whenever Beatrice is in the room. Beatrice wears more flattering clothes these days, too. Beatrice doesn't talk about it, but they seem to make a good match."

"After what happened with her last boyfriend, I'd say she needs some time. Best to take it slow. Give me Jasper's number when you get a chance."

❄ ❄ ❄

Judge Terri Cromwell entered the reception area of the Peabody Mansion. The wedding décor dazzled the senses: sparkling snowflakes falling from the ceiling, a massive tree decorated with white ornaments and twinkling lights, and the white glitter table clothes created the perfect ambiance for a winter wedding.

"Good morning. I'm Kim Stokes, the assistant manager. How may I help you?"

"I'm Terri Cromwell, here to meet with Autumn."

"Oh! Judge Cromwell! Welcome!"

"Thank you, dear. Who's responsible for this wedding wonderland?"

"Our resident party planner and décor specialist, Elizabeth Johnson."

"Is she available for other venues?"

"Yes, but if you're holding a party, consider having it here. We'll officially open in January," said Kim proudly.

"Autumn chose the right representative for the Peabody Mansion," Terri smiled at her. "I'll certainly keep it in mind."

Autumn came down the winding white marble staircase, the queen of her castle, dressed in dark-wash jeans and a gold cable-knit sweater that went perfectly with her long, auburn hair. She cradled Chrissy in her arms, the bright eyes showing from beneath her long, silky hair, the princess of this domain.

"Good morning!" said Autumn cheerfully.

"Good morning. What a place! Kim and I were talking about having my next event here. She's quite the salesperson."

Kim's pale skin took on a reddish hue at the compliment.

"Great job, Kim!" Autumn beamed at her. Then to Terri she said, "Kim earned a promotion to assistant manager. I knew I picked the right woman."

Kim glowed at Autumn's kind words.

Terri started taking her coat off, but Autumn stopped her. "We're heading outside first, and then we'll come in and finish our meeting," she said, donning her coat and fully outfitting Chrissy. "I want you to check out the amazing job Elizabeth did outside."

"A woman of many talents!"

"You have no idea. You weren't here for the Halloween party. Elizabeth outdid herself."

Autumn waved her fingers at Kim as they headed out the door. Ward stood near the trailhead, sweeping the latest dusting of snow from the path. He tipped his hat.

"Ladies," he greeted.

"Hi Ward. This is Judge Cromwell. She's presiding over the ceremony."

He held out his gloved hand. "Judge."

She shook it with her gloved hand. The weather was too cold to remove the layer of protection from the frigid air.

"Ward. Nice to meet you."

"He's in charge of everything having to do with the property and the building. Ward built our hay bale maze at Halloween and is an essential part of the success of this wedding." Autumn patted his arm.

He bowed his head in thanks.

"Hello little girl," he bent down to pet Chrissy. She wagged her tail at him.

"Ward is responsible for positioning the statuary. He works with Elizabeth to create the effect you're about to see."

"I've never seen Foo Dogs this large. It must have been quite an undertaking."

"Yes, ma'am," Ward agreed.

"Thanks, Ward," said Autumn, leading the judge between the Foo Dogs and down the path.

They walked past the statuary and down to the Sycamore.

"You'll stand in front of the tree. Ward is installing outdoor heaters and draping for this area, so don't worry about the cold."

"You've thought of everything."

"Well, Elizabeth deserves the credit. She's very thorough." She pointed to either side of the clearing. "The chairs for guests will be placed here and here."

"This is really amazing, Autumn. How many people are coming?"

"We sent 100 invitations. With weather and scheduling conflicts, I'm not sure. We're still receiving RSVPs. I believe those meant to be here will be."

"Healthy attitude."

Autumns smiled. "I only care about marrying Ray. The rest is very nice, but spending the rest of my life with him is what's important to me."

Chrissy let out a single, sharp bark.

"She either agrees with me or she's cold." Autumn picked up her furry little bundle and snuggled her close. Chrissy nestled against her mommy's neck.

They went back inside to a table set up with a choice of tea or hot chocolate and made themselves comfortable in the study. Chrissy sat next to Autumn on the couch.

"I want to apologize, again, for my son, Barry."

"Please don't give it another thought."

But Judge Cromwell continued.

"He lives in a residential treatment center in the Poconos. As you observed, he's hard to manage. Angela Curry diagnosed his schizophrenia and recommended he live where they understand his illness. The care team there stays on top of his medications and behavioral outbursts."

Autumn sipped her cocoa, nodding. "It must be difficult for both of you."

"It is. He loved Dr. Curry. Not just as his psychologist. She texted me after his last session and told me he made inappropriate advances toward her."

"What did she do about it?"

"Told him she couldn't treat him anymore."

"When did this happen?"

"During this visit home. He's been angry and acting out since her death. Actually, I think it was the day the police said she died."

Autumn felt alarm bells going off. She wasn't sure Ray had Barry on his suspect list.

"Maybe he could talk to Ray and give him some details about the timeline. It could help the case."

Terri Cromwell sipped her herbal tea and frowned.

"I'll suggest it to him before he goes back to the treatment center."

"When is that?"

"In a few days."

"Ray can swing by your house to speak with him, if that's easier."

Terri sighed with relief.

"That would be better. Then it won't turn into a confrontation. Barry doesn't like me so much these days. I just can't handle him physically."

"I'll call Ray and ask him to bring an officer with him, just in case."

"If they're in plain clothes, that would be best to avoid setting him off."

After Autumn relayed to Ray what Terri said, the judge frowned.

"I'm sorry, Autumn. I've worried about this since I heard Chrissy found the body."

Chrissy looked up at the sound of her name. Autumn kissed her head and stroked her back.

"Yes, you, my little detective."

Chrissy put her head back down.

"When I went to a therapist for PTSD, he gave me a coping strategy that might work for you."

"Let's try it," said Terri.

"Feel your feet on the floor. Be in this moment. Not the future and not the past."

Terri closed her eyes.

Autumn continued. "There is only us. This room is the only thing that exists. Take a deep breath in, still feeling your feet on the floor, and let it out."

She instructed her to take two more deep breaths.

"How do you feel?"

Terri opened her eyes slowly.

"Calmer. Centered." Terri looked around. "I like this room with the old hardback books and the fireplace. If I had to pick a room to be the only one in the world, this would be it." She smiled.

Autumn smiled back. "Yes, this is my favorite room in the mansion. It's cozy. The dark green walls feel like they're hugging me."

"Yes!" Terri agreed. "Thank you." All the same, she still looked concerned and wrung her hands.

"What's wrong?"

Terri said, "I know we're less than a week away from the wedding, so it pains me to say this. With Barry now potentially involved with this murder and Ray brought in to investigate, ethically, I need to withdraw myself from presiding over your wedding or even attending. People may view it as an impropriety. I want my integrity and your wedding pristine."

"I'm sorry to hear that, but I understand," said Autumn sadly. "How about Josh Snyder?"

"The mayor of Knollwood?"

"Sure, he's qualified."

"And he's also on the guest list already, so it won't seem so last-minute to include him."

"I'll call him and explain the situation so you don't have to."

"Thank you, Terri. I hope everything works out for the best for Barry."

"Me, too."

They hugged and Chrissy got tickled under the chin.

"I'll see you soon, sweetheart," Terri said affectionately.

Chrissy made a throaty little sound in agreement.

≈15≈

Who knew half the town was in therapy? Ray was shocked at the list from Dr. Curry's attorney, Jodi Fallston, without session notes. It read like a suspect list if he ever saw one. There were some surprises, too. Brittany Farmer's therapy didn't seem to do her any good given the recent sabotage of his wedding. Megan Harris, who'd given Brittany information on Autumn's wedding gown, had also sought help from Dr. Angela Curry. He knew about Harry Halifax and William Moore.

And now, a call from Autumn about Barry Cromwell, on Dr. Curry's client list and his mother concerned about his last appointment with her.

Had Dr. Curry undermined the recovery of her clients? After all, she threatened Harry Halifax about their affair.

He thanked his lucky stars that Autumn's treatment by a reputable psychologist healed her rather than someone like Curry, whose clients took actions that made their lives worse.

Faith Halifax wasn't on the list, but her connection to Dr. Curry through her husband kept her top-of-mind as a murder suspect. He was on his way to see her when he got the call from Autumn about Barry Cromwell. He dialed Chief Stanley to get a plain-clothes officer to go with him. It was still their case, but Ray had permission to investigate, since they were shorthanded, and he included them as much as possible.

The one thing he hadn't shared with the chief related to William Moore's lack of follow-up. Ray wanted to see where that led.

Officer Jim Osgood showed up wearing street clothes that showed his muscular physique. At over six feet tall, he was intimidating without saying a word. Ray had worked with him on a case a few years back and found him diligent and trustworthy.

And Ace liked him. Jim held out his hand to Ace and petted him.

"How are you, buddy?"

Ace let out one sharp bark, making Jim smile.

Ray explained the situation and Barry's mental health status to Jim, to prepare him for a potential physical altercation.

Ray knocked on Judge Cromwell's door. Ace was in a guarding position next to him. Jim stood slightly behind them and to the side.

"I'll go around back," he said.

Ray nodded and knocked again. The sound of feet running down the hallway echoed inside the house and through the front door.

"Barry Cromwell?" Ray shouted through the door.

No answer.

Ray went around back to find Jim Osgood restraining Barry by the scruff of his collar. Barry fought against him, but Jim held tight. Ace barked and snarled, spraying saliva toward Barry.

"Hey, Barry," said Ray. "We just want to ask you a few questions. Is that okay?"

"No! Get that dog away from me!" Barry screamed and continued to fight Jim.

Ray gave Ace a signal to quiet down and stand watch. Ace complied, but showed his teeth and growled deep in his throat. He acted more upset than Ray had ever seen before.

"We just want to talk to you about Dr. Curry," Ray assured him.

"She's gone!" Barry cried.

"That's true. Can you tell us about that?" Ray said gently.

"Dr. Curry!" Barry yelled as though she were across the street.

"My name is Ray, this is Jim, and the German shepherd is Ace. How about we go back into the house and talk? You can tell us all about what happened to her."

Barry stopped battling against Jim.

Ray signaled to Jim to get him back in the house. They walked him up the back steps and into the kitchen. Ace brought up the rear.

Barry paced and grumbled.

Ray saw pill bottles lined up along on the counter.

"Hey, Barry, are any of these yours?"

He stopped and nodded, then continued pacing.

"Is it time for your medication?"

Barry shrugged over and over while he paced.

Ray called Autumn to contact the judge and see if Barry should take any of these meds. Terri Cromwell called Ray back within minutes and gave him instructions. After studying the array of medications, Ray pulled one pill each from two different bottles and gave them to Barry with a glass of water.

Barry swallowed the pills and handed the glass back to Ray. It seemed a rote movement after years of treatment. Jim stood by the door ready to block an attempted escape, and Ray waited near the sink until the medication took effect and Barry calmed down.

"Here you go," Ray said, pulling out a chair.

Barry stared at Ace, who didn't budge, and then sat. Ray positioned himself at a right angle to Barry.

"How are you feeling?"

Barry shrugged. "OK, I guess."

"Good. Can we talk about Dr. Curry?"

Barry's face scrunched up like he was ready to cry, but no tears came.

"She's gone!"

"Yes, she is," said Ray in a soothing voice.

"It's my fault!" Barry hit himself in the head with an open palm.

"Tell me what happened."

"She told me I couldn't see her anymore."

"And then what?"

"I got so mad!" Barry growled.

"Did you hurt Dr. Curry?"

"I don't know. I can't remember."

"Do you remember stabbing her?"

"I don't know!" Barry screamed, his face red and sweaty. He punched himself harder.

"Maybe we could take him to the hospital and have a psychiatrist question him," suggested Jim.

Ray looked over at him. "Good idea."

"Bucks County Memorial has a psych unit."

Ray turned to Barry. "Will you come with us to the hospital?"

Barry slumped with exhaustion. "OK."

When the woman came into the reception area, Kim called for Autumn. She was in the living room with Elizabeth and Beatrice, decorating the fifteen-foot-tall artificial tree. Chrissy sniffed the ornaments and reached out gently with her silky paw. She wore a glittering white bow in her topknot. Autumn watched her for safety reasons, knowing Chrissy wasn't destructive, but might get curious about how something inedible might taste.

The tree would welcome guests at the inn's grand opening and stay up through winter. Elizabeth planned to put Christmas ornaments on it for the holidays. Autumn loved the idea of using the Peabody family antique ornaments that hadn't seen a merry Christmas for decades. Then she'd go back to a winter theme that didn't feel like a wedding.

They cleared a space to store the massive tree in the attic with the Christmas decorations.

Autumn came out and greeted the woman. She kept her snow jacket, scarf, pompom knit hat, and gloves on.

"How can I help you?"

"I'm Faith Halifax. Do you have a few minutes to talk about the ice sculpture?"

"Of course, please come with me."

She walked Faith into the vast living room. The Palladian window framed the snow-covered woods.

Faith looked around, a look of awe on her face, but said nothing.

"This is where we're holding the reception."

Elizabeth looked up and came over.

"Hi, Faith. How are you?" said Elizabeth, reaching out to shake hands.

Faith kept her hand gloved and at her side.

"Well, thanks. It's good to see you."

Elizabeth said to Autumn, "We met at Harry's studio when I ordered the sculpture."

"And then canceled it and then reordered."

Autumn sensed resentment in Faith's tone.

"Sadly, circumstances required it, but we're glad we can do business with you now. I'm sure you understand," Autumn said.

"I could have called, but I wanted to see the look on your face. You'll have to do without an ice sculpture at your wedding."

Autumn and Elizabeth looked at each other.

"My husband's art is valuable, and for him to put time and creativity into something for a couple who accused him of murder is unforgivable!" said Faith, crossing her arms and lifting her chin in defiance.

"A murder investigation is a special circumstance. That you're offended by Harry being a suspect is out of line," said Autumn.

Chrissy trotted over and looked at her mommy and then at Faith. Autumn picked her up and rubbed her back. The furry munchkin didn't take well to conflict and aggression.

"I know he didn't do it," said Faith.

"You may want to share whatever you know with the police," said Autumn, understanding why Faith would defend her husband.

"He didn't need to kill her. Not for my sake!"

Autumn paused.

"Are you saying that Harry did it?"

"I'm saying that he has affairs with a lot of women. They mean nothing to him. Why would he worry about his affair with Angela Curry?" Faith put her face in her hands, and then looked up at Autumn.

No tears streaked her cheeks.

Autumn sensed Faith's instability and handed Chrissy to Elizabeth for safekeeping. Elizabeth took a couple of steps back as she cradled Chrissy close to her chest.

"It must be hard to deal with his infidelity," Autumn empathized, having had her own experiences with betrayal in the past. Thank goodness Ray was trustworthy. Besides, his mother would have him for lunch if he pulled something like that.

"He leaves me alone and has his one-night stands. But this one wanted him all to herself!"

Faith's anger grew as she told her story of a dysfunctional marriage.

"How do you know that?"

"She called me and told me she's stealing my husband. That they're in love!" Faith's clenched fists straining the leather of her gloves.

Autumn turned her head toward Elizabeth and mouthed "call Ray."

Elizabeth backed away and left the room with Chrissy snuggled against her neck.

"Did you confront Harry?"

Faith shook her head.

"No. She needed to be taught a lesson, not Harry!"

Autumn sat in the window seat and patted the cushion next to her.

"You're upset. Sit with me," said Autumn gently.

Faith snapped her head toward Autumn as though coming out of a trance, then turned and raced through the reception area and out the front door.

Elizabeth came back into the room and handed Chrissy to her mommy. Autumn took her and kissed her head.

"No ice sculpture is worth this craziness," said Elizabeth.

Autumn looked at her, eyebrows raised.

"It's not, right?"

Autumn smiled.

❊ ❊ ❊

"Is she still there?" Ray asked from his SUV.

"No, but Ray, she knew about Harry's affair."

"Harry told me she knew nothing about it."

"Well, she did. She knows about all of his affairs."

"I'll have to see her after we finish with Barry."

"How is he?"

"Medicated. We're on our way to the hospital to have a psychiatrist interview him and check his condition. He may have been hallucinating earlier. It was like he saw Angela Curry and called out to her."

"It must be hard to have a condition like that. Chrissy went after him when we visited the judge's house."

"Ace went crazy."

"Ray, the wedding is a week away, and I'm not comfortable dealing with Harry and Faith Halifax."

"I'd rather you didn't at this point."

"How disappointed would you be if we didn't have an ice sculpture at the wedding reception?"

Ray burst out laughing.

"I think we'll be fine without it."

❊ ❊ ❊

Pamela Brown drummed her fingers against the desk, eyes fixed on the cursor of her laptop, blinking on a clean, white page. She tapped the screen of her phone, hoping she'd see a missed call from one of her sources. Nothing.

She'd been through dry periods in the past, but not during a murder investigation. All the information on the wedding of the year had also gone silent. She confirmed the rumor of Megan's closed shop and departure by calling the realtor, Maureen Roberts, inquiring about the properties.

Pamela's fans demanded a steady stream of local dirt, but cut off from her informants, her flow stopped. William Moore, Brittany Farmer, and Megan Harris had all disappeared. The betrayal stung her to the core. She had to find another way to get the information on the murder suspects and the wedding.

She'd already tried Elizabeth Johnson and Kim Stokes, but they refused. The other two close to Autumn, were Beatrice Peabody and Ward Everly, both brutally loyal and impossible to sway. The wedding vendors had clammed up, as well, warned about sharing information by Elizabeth. They couldn't take the chance of losing future business. The Peabody Mansion B&B stood to be one of the premier event venues in the area, and shop owners and service providers wanted its business.

Pamela tapped her pen against the lined pad next to her computer, trying to come up with people close to the situation but without loyalty to Autumn Clarke and Ray Reed. Then she'd put together a plan to trick them into giving up information.

=16=

The psychiatrist at the hospital impressed Ray. Dr. Tim O'Brien took them right away and had already called the treatment center to find out more about Barry's condition, medications, and therapy.

"I understand you'd like to help Barry remember an altercation with his therapist."

"That's correct. Barry's recollection will help us in the murder investigation."

"Is he a suspect?"

"Possibly, but we won't know until we determine how accurately he remembers his last encounter with the victim and what happened the night she died."

"Right now, we're doing bloodwork and a psych eval. It's best to get him stabilized before questioning."

"You or a staff member can question him, as long as we're in the room. If you can get the story about the night Dr. Curry died and anything Barry might have seen, we'd appreciate it."

"Got it. We'll be ready in about 90 minutes.

"I'll be back then."

❄ ❄ ❄

Ray pulled up to Halifax Designs, hoping Faith was at the studio. He leashed Ace and helped him to the ground.

"Be alert," Ray told him.

Ace made a muffled bark in response.

They set off a buzzer when entering the sparse promotional area with black-framed photos of Harry's ice sculptures hung on bright white walls, brochures describing ordering and pricing, and an unpainted timber shelf displaying Harry's national and international ice art competition trophies. Ray heard banging and sawing coming from the back of the building.

A door off to the side opened, and Faith entered. She took a step back when she saw Ray leaning against the counter with his hand tucked in his pants pocket, and Ace standing at attention, his dark, shining eyes fixed on her.

"Hi, Faith."

"Ray, I, uh... how can I help you?"

"Mind if I ask you a few questions?"

"Depends. Is it business?"

"No. Autumn and I understand your position and won't order anything now or in the future."

"Oh, uh..."

"So, there's no conflict of interest to ask about the night of Dr. Curry's murder."

Faith realized her mouth hung open and snapped her jaw shut. "I see. Do I need an attorney?"

"That's up to you."

With no reply one way or the other, Ray asked, "Mind if we sit?"

Ray and Ace moved toward the mid-century modern dining set with a round wooden table, bright yellow chairs, and a photo album of ice sculpture designs. The chair scraped across the dull linoleum floor. He gestured for Ace to sit next to him.

Faith reluctantly joined them, pulling out a chair opposite Ray and the farthest from Ace. She folded her weathered, unadorned hands on top of the table.

Ray pulled a small notebook and a pen from his inside jacket pocket. He noticed Faith's bangs stuck to her forehead. The sounds coming from the workshop continued as a backdrop.

"Where were you the night Dr. Curry died?"

"Home."

"Was anyone with you between 6 pm and 10 pm?"

"No."

"Where was Harry?"

Faith paused. "I don't know."

"What time did you expect him back?"

"I never know when he's coming home. He's a free spirit."

"What time was it when he returned?"

"Around 10 or 10:30, I guess."

"How did he seem when he got home?"

Faith pressed her lips together. "Angry. Agitated."

"About what?"

"I didn't ask."

"Why not? Don't you care how your husband feels?"

"I'm not his keeper!" Faith snapped and looked down at her hands.

Ray made a note, thinking that Autumn would want to know that he was okay and if she could help.

"What did he do when he got home?"

"Went to his studio. That's where he works through things that bother him."

"What did you do?"

"Went to his van to bring his tools in. Someone has stolen them before. A lot of good the police are in this town."

Ray pushed away a grimace. "Did you report it?"

"Well, uh, no. We weren't sure when they went missing. Harry didn't know if he locked the van."

He looked at Faith until she met his eyes. "If you don't report it, the police won't know there's a problem."

She nodded, defeated. "Ever since that happened, I check the van and remove the tools when he gets home."

"Was anything missing?"

"No, but, uh, never mind."

Ray waited.

Faith rubbed her hands on her pants, just as Harry did during questioning. Ray wondered if he and Autumn would take on one another's behavioral habits the way Faith and Harry had.

She took a deep breath. "All the tools were there, but one wasn't in his carry bag where he usually keeps it. And there was blood on it."

"Which tool is that, Faith?"

"The ten-inch chipper tool."

"You didn't think to report it?"

"Harry cuts himself all the time. I figured it was his blood."

"What did you do with it?"

"What I do with all his tools. Scrubbed it clean and put it back in its place in his workshop."

"I'd like you to show me that tool. I'll need to take it as evidence."

She nodded.

"You mentioned to Autumn that Dr. Curry called you and said she wanted to break up your marriage. Is that true?"

"Yes," she whispered.

"How did that make you feel?"

"What is this? A therapy session?"

"When did Dr. Curry call you?"

"The night before you found her. In the afternoon."

"Did you kill Dr. Curry?"

"No!" Faith's composure burst. She pushed her chair away from the table, stood, and screamed, "Get out!"

Ace was on his feet, growling and baring his teeth.

Ray stood up.

"I'll need the tool you described first."

Harry poked his head through the door.

"Everything okay?"

"Mr. Halifax, your wife just admitted to finding blood on one of your tools. I need to take it with me."

Harry looked at Faith. "You found blood on my tools?"

Faith boiled and didn't answer.

"She said she'd cleaned it and put it back in your workshop. Mrs. Halifax, you'll need to show us which one."

They went to the studio. The chipper tool hung in its spot on the wall. Faith reached for it, but Ray beat her to it with a glove and plastic evidence bag.

Sealing the bag, he said, "I'll be in touch. You may want to hire a lawyer."

☆17☆

Judge Cromwell jumped into her car and sped towards the hospital where her son waited to be questioned. Ray's text made her stomach knot and her mind race with the possibility her son had committed murder. She wanted to know the extent of his violent nature. Sadness washed over her, but didn't cleanse the anxiety that took over her entire body.

Was it her fault for letting him come home to visit? Would Barry have to move to a permanent in-patient facility?

She trusted Lieutenant Ray Reed and knew of his meticulous investigative skills. If Barry was innocent, Ray would clear his name. If guilty, Ray would make sure justice prevailed.

Her cell phone rang. She punched the screen to answer and greeted the caller on speaker.

"Hello, Judge Cromwell. This is Detective William Moore."

"Yes, Detective, how can I help you?"

"I understand your son is being held at Bucks County hospital in the psych ward."

Distrust welled up from the depths of her being. Law enforcement personnel rarely called her directly.

"Is this your case, Detective?"

"I was working on it before Ray Reed took it over. I'm hoping you'll put me back on the case."

"For what reason?"

"Ray Reed already went after your son. He'll ruin everyone's lives if he continues in this direction."

"I'll keep it in mind, Detective Moore," said the judge, and disconnected the call.

❄ ❄ ❄

More snow fell on the sleepy Knollwood neighborhood. The fire crackled in the den, making the snowy day warm and cozy. Chrissy lay with her feet behind her, front paws grasping her favorite non-rawhide treat, head tilted to the side, happily working it with her back teeth. She stopped chewing when Autumn came in with a box holding an evergreen garland and smiled at her mommy.

"What do you have, my darling? Is that good?" Autumn cooed.

Chrissy wagged her tail and went back to chewing.

The focus on wedding plans and murder took her away from her usual routine of decorating the house. Her mother, Stella, always made everything just so for Christmas. She insisted on a fresh evergreen garland on the mantle for both the smell and to nestle the stockings hanging from hooks hidden in the needles.

Autumn crowned the garland with her mother's favorite ornaments. The glittered balls sparkled in the firelight.

Ray and Adam had installed the root ball of the live tree into a rustic container in the corner of the den, away from the fireplace. Ward Everly volunteered to plant the tree after the New Year. He guided them as to the need to keep the tree cool, then put it in the garage to transition it before being planted outside. This gave it the best chance of surviving. Autumn wasn't sure if she wanted it on her home's property or to add it to the forest at the mansion. There was plenty of time to decide.

Her home. Their home. The thought made her heart lift.

The quiet offered Autumn a break from the stress of late. Part of her wanted to decorate the tree alone, accompanied by the happy memories of her childhood Christmases. The house filled with laughter and her parents perfectly partnered to make the tree look perfect. Over the years, the décor transitioned from silver strings of tinsel hanging from the branches to wide green velvet ribbons strung in loops.

That was the last embellishment Stella Clarke made before the car accident that took her life and the life of Autumn's father, George. Autumn survived the crash with minor injuries and major PTSD. Focusing on the happy memories of her parents in the quiet afternoon made it feel like they were still with her. The green velvet ribbon had a place on this tree and every tree yet to come. But sadly, it wouldn't be Stella and George hanging it.

Autumn pictured a scene with Ray meeting her parents for the first time and having everyone excited that she found the love of her life. The thought made her smile. A powerful vision astoundingly made it feel authentic enough to make her smile.

This being the first Christmas they were all together, Autumn had stockings made for Chrissy, Ray, and Ace to hang along with hers. She'd fill them with fun little gifts: chocolate and a new black leather, pocket-sized notebook for Ray to replace the filled and peeling one he currently used, delicious snacks for the pups, a new ball for Chrissy, and a large chew toy for Ace, among other things. In her mind, the stockings were the most fun to fill and unwrap.

Tonight was the first time decorating the tree with her new family members. Ray's parents were great and wanted to be involved, which Autumn loved. The hot cocoa and wine would supplement whatever Carol Reed was bringing for dinner. She insisted, which was fine with Autumn.

She sat in the deep cushioned chair, gazing at her work. Chrissy saw a snuggle opportunity and leaped onto the chair and pushed down between Autumn's leg and the arm of the chair.

"I love sitting with you," Autumn said, straightening Chrissy's green satin bows.

Chrissy put her head across Autumn's thigh and sighed.

"You're my special present every single day," said Autumn, picking up Chrissy and kissing her face.

Chrissy licked her check and nuzzled against her neck.

They sat in the peaceful room, the only world that existed, in a bubble of love.

When the fire turned to embers, Autumn lifted her little treasure and put her on the floor.

"Let's make some room for Daddy!"

Autumn headed to the master bedroom, with Chrissy trotting behind.

The renovated room was sage green. A tapestry bedspread and big fluffy pillows welcomed Chrissy as Autumn lifted her and sat her on the bed. The sweet pup laid her head on her mommy's pillow and closed her eyes.

Autumn had already donated most of her parents' clothing, leaving a seven-foot-long closet with shelves and racks empty for Ray's stuff. Autumn's clothing filled her mother's walk-in closet. Chrissy had her own little cabinet with drawers for bows and brushes and a little rack for her jackets and dresses. Autumn went through the dresser drawers, condensing her items and making sure Ray had plenty of space.

"All done, sweetheart!"

Chrissy looked up, lazily wagging her tail.

"I guess Ace's bed will go on Ray's side."

No need to place Chrissy's bed since she had them in different rooms, but she slept through the night in Autumn's bed and would continue to do so.

Clapping her hands in excitement and joy at the pending merger of living space, she picked up Chrissy and went to the second floor, where there were three bedrooms. Autumn's office was yellow and at the end of the hall. She had emptied the one at the top of the stairs for Ray's office. He chose a deep gray for his space, saying it would look good with his steel and glass desk. The third bedroom was up for grabs. Autumn's old queen bed was in there, but easily moved out. They'd decide its function together. Maybe an exercise room.

"We're all set, sweetheart," Autumn said with a glowing smile.

☙18☙

Barry sat in an armchair in Dr. O'Brien's office, his posture relaxed from the cocktail of medications. Ray watched unobtrusively from across the room. Ace sat at attention beside him.

"Barry, I'd like to ask you a few questions about Dr. Curry," said Dr. O'Brien.

Barry's dull eyes seemed unseeing. He grunted his reply.

"Do you remember the last time you saw Dr. Curry?"

Barry nodded.

"Did you have a fight with her?"

Another affirmative nod.

"Was she hurt when you left her office?"

Barry's eyes closed halfway.

"Barry?"

His eyed snapped wider and then went back to half-mast.

Ray spoke up.

"Do you really think he's well enough to respond? The drugs seem too potent to allow accurate recall."

"To tell you the truth, Lieutenant, his condition is severe. His aptitude for violence requires this level of medication."

"Based on what?"

"Well, your Detective Moore said you told him to tell me everything about this patient."

"What did he say?"

"That he saw Barry strike Dr. Curry."

Ray pressed his lips together, holding in his frustration.

"Dry him out, Dr. O'Brien. If he becomes agitated, give him something mild, but keep him lucid."

"That will take until tomorrow."

Ray left the room, determined to find William Moore and dress him down. Ace kept pace with him out to the SUV. The SUV slid on the snowy parking lot pavement as Ray peeled out, heading to the Chief's office to file a formal complaint.

❄ ❄ ❄

"I haven't seen him, Ray," said the New Hope Police Chief.

"In the years I've known Moore, I never thought he'd deliberately sabotage a case."

"He hasn't been in the last few days. When we last spoke, he said you asked him to look into finding Brittany Farmer and to get off the Angela Curry case."

"That's true, because he was a patient of Dr. Curry's."

Bruce Stanley looked at Ray over steepled fingers.

"I forgot about that. It seems he feels like you demoted him. He even called Judge Cromwell to advocate for him to get put back on the case. Maybe he figured by talking to the psychiatrist, he would win over the judge."

"It's possible. But I'm trying to learn what Barry Cromwell knows, and his interference delayed that."

The police chief nodded.

"Let's not put in a formal complaint just yet. I'll try contacting him and see what this is all about."

"I appreciate that, Chief."

"How're the wedding plans coming along? I sent in my RSVP. The wife is looking forward to it."

"Mostly fine. There have been some hiccups along the way. We've decided not to have an ice sculpture given the potential involvement of Harry and Faith Halifax in Dr. Curry's murder."

Chief Stanley laughed.

"I've never known you to compromise your ethics, Ray. It's one thing I like about you."

He looked down at Ace.

"And you're the other thing."

Ace gave a single, sharp bark.

Ray and Ace stopped home to clean up before heading to Autumn's house. The houseful of boxes made his life feel temporary. He looked forward to getting settled after the wedding. They'd honeymoon after that. The important thing was to get their new situation in order.

Autumn made him feel it was their house, despite having lived there all her life. The office room was perfect for when he wanted to work from home. He had way more space there than in his small apartment. One of Ace's beds would go in there, too, so his buddy could sit with him.

He hoped Chrissy wouldn't feel intruded upon by Ace living there full time. They got along well, but the little girl was used to some alone time with her mommy. With him working most of the time, they'd both be out of the house, so it would balance itself out.

The low water pressure of the shower made him clean, but not relaxed. Autumn's plumbing was better. Thinking of the house as theirs was a challenge. It would take some time to acclimate to the idea.

He ran a brush through Ace to freshen him up and threw handfuls of dog hair into the trash.

"Looking good, Ace!!"

Ace wagged his tail.

This was the first tree he'd decorated in years. His mother was excited. Her love of Autumn made things much easier on their relationship. After all, you marry the family, not just the individual.

❄ ❄ ❄

Carol and Kevin Reed beat Ray to the house. They stamped their feet to loosen the snow from their boots and wiped them on the mat inside before taking them off. Autumn welcomed them with open arms after taking the large pot of soup from Kevin's hands and let him help Carol with the casserole dish.

"Boy, it's really coming down out there," said Kevin.

"Warm the soup on low heat and the casserole on two hundred fifty degrees. It's cooked. We just want to make the mushroom soup smooth," said Carol, pulling out slippers from her jumbo bag and handing a pair to Kevin.

Chrissy got on her hind legs and batted Carol's knee.

"Hello, sweetheart!"

Carol picked her up and cradled her. Kevin scratched behind her ears.

"You're going to be my grand-pup!" Carol gave her a gentle squeeze. Chrissy made a low rumble of contentment.

"I hope the weather holds out for the wedding," Kevin said.

"I trust everything will happen the way it's supposed to," said Autumn, loading the casserole dish into the oven.

"Where's Ray?" Carol asked, putting Chrissy down.

"He stopped at his apartment to change."

Kevin asked, "Why didn't he change here?"

"He's welcome to, but he has this thing about living together before we're official. Something to do with the last time he lived with someone and having it not work out."

"Patty Myers," said Kevin, rolling his eyes. He dipped a celery stick into ranch dressing and chomped down. "She was a piece of work. Never knew what he saw in her."

"No matter," said Carol, "He picked wisely this time." She put her arm around Autumn and gave her a little hug.

Autumn beamed.

"How about some wine?"

"I'm not sure with the weather the way it is," said Kevin. "Carol can have some."

"We have a guest room upstairs. You're welcome to stay over."

And just like that, the unassigned room became a guest room. The queen-sized bed moved from what was now Ray's office would serve for now. She could make it even cozier going forward. It would take minutes to make the bed.

Kevin grabbed a goblet and smiled. "Then pour away!"

Autumn served them and herself. She fed Chrissy while the food was heating. She loved the munching and lapping sounds Chrissy made when enjoying her food.

"Hey, guys!" Ray said. He kissed his mom on the cheek and hugged his dad. He kissed Autumn on the mouth, making it brief enough with an audience present. Chrissy was at his feet, tail metronome quick.

"Hey, there, little one." He rubbed her neck.

Ace came charging in, wagging his tail.

"Did he eat yet?" asked Autumn.

"Yes, but I'm sure he'd love a snack."

Autumn showed Ace and Chrissy their snack choices, each selecting their favorite and taking it into the den to enjoy.

"The roads are really slick," Ray said, pouring himself a glass of Chianti.

"That's why we're having a sleepover party. You can all relax, eat, drink..."

"Where will my parents sleep?"

"The new guest room upstairs," Autumn smiled.

"Great idea! I'll help you make up the bed."

"Not before we eat, you won't," said Carol, checking the casserole and then stirring the soup.

"I'll stoke the fire," Kevin offered.

Autumn set the dining room table and placed trivets in the center.

Carol used oven mitts to carry the steaming hot tuna casserole, complete with crispy fried onions on the top.

"My mom used to make this for me. Brings back happy memories."

"I'm glad, dear."

They put the soup in a tureen with a matching ladle and placed it on the other trivet. Baskets of freshly baked croissants and thick multi-grain bread and butter at either end of the table rounded out the meal.

Autumn lit the green and red holiday candles she saved for a special occasion.

"You set a lovely table, Autumn," said Carol, admiring the scene.

When everyone took their seats, Autumn raised her glass. Ace lay content on the floor next to Ray, and Chrissy curled up near Autumn's chair.

"Thank you for being here and making this holiday and the wedding so special. Being part of your family is a special honor for Chrissy and me. I love you all."

"We're the lucky ones," said Ray, reaching for her hand and squeezing it.

"To love and luck!" toasted Carol.

They clinked glasses.

Conversation was amusing and light. Dinner was delicious. The snowflakes kept coming, making a storybook scene outside the picture window in the den. And the tree looked beautiful.

Hot cocoa ended the night. Kevin added some peppermint schnapps to his cup. The others followed suit. Good thing they slept over. Besides, it would take all of them to shovel out in the morning.

It was a relief to find the roads to the Peabody Mansion plowed and salted. Autumn still took it slow and made sure she secured Chrissy in her car seat. Ward had cleared the driveway and parking area.

"What would I do without you?" she asked him, who was sprinkling dog-friendly ice-melt on the steps.

"Let's not find out," Ward answered, smiling.

He put the bag down and removed his glove to pet Chrissy.

"Hey, there, young lady."

Chrissy wagged her tail and then went to find a suitable spot to relieve herself.

"Will you bring a guest to the wedding?"

"I'm not sure."

"It's getting close. We have you down for two, no matter what."

"I appreciate that."

Autumn patted him on the shoulder. Chrissy charged up the steps toward the front door and Autumn followed.

The heat hit them as soon as they entered. The clicking of the radiators soothed Autumn's nerves.

"There you are!" said Bea, marching from the living room to the reception area.

"Hi, Bea. How does everything look?"

"I'm concerned about the candles on the mantle."

"What about them?"

"They sputtered."

"Like flickered?"

"Yes. It means evil spirits are lurking."

Autumn knew better than to challenge the premise that evil spirits and not a draft made the candles flicker.

"Well, Judge Cromwell can't marry us because of the murder investigation."

Bea pointed her finger at Autumn, jabbing it toward her.

"See! Cursed!"

"The good news is that Mayor Josh Snyder agreed to perform the ceremony." Autumn did a little celebration jig, complete with fist pumps.

"That's because I ordered the candy-coated almonds as a safeguard."

"I'm sure that's why it worked out."

Autumn hugged her. Bea meant well.

Chrissy barked for Bea's attention.

"Was I ignoring you?" asked Bea and lifted Chrissy into her arms and gave her a squeeze. "You're so good."

They walked into the living room. It looked like a winter wonderland. Elizabeth was in the corner, putting the finishing touches on the tree.

"Looks beautiful, Elizabeth!" Autumn called across the room.

"It does! I'm thrilled with how it turned out," Elizabeth said.

"Remember to put your cards around the reception area."

"That's too blatant, isn't it?"

"I could make an announcement thanking you for your work."

"This is your wedding, for goodness' sakes. How about we wait until someone asks for my card?"

Autumn thought about it.

"Fine, and have your cards on the reception desk."

"Deal."

"And take lots of pictures for your portfolio."

Elizabeth laughed. "You should have been in public relations. I can't wait for the bachelorette party. After all this work, I could use a massage."

"I've been thinking about that," said Bea. "In Finland, it's customary for the bride to have a sauna with her ladies the day before the wedding."

"How about two days before?"

"I guess that would work," said Bea.

"Why is that?" asked Elizabeth.

"It's part of a beauty ritual and preparing for the next stage of life. It's also a symbol of giving up her former life."

"So sweat it out, eh?" Autumn laughed.

"I think it's better to have it two days before. That steam can't be good for our hairdos. It'll give us a day to recover and then have our hair done."

"I've arranged for all the ladies to have makeup and hair at *Jolie Salon* on Main Street the morning of the wedding," said Autumn.

"I'm not in the wedding party," said Elizabeth.

"No, but you created the party, so you're in."

"Are they doing Chrissy's hair, too?"

"I have a groomer coming here when we get back from the salon to do her hair and secure her collar ornament."

"The photographer is all set. I also have a videographer coming," Elizabeth told them.

"Glad I have you to think of these things."

"You shouldn't have to. You've got enough going on."

"True. I have to make a call. You ladies have everything in hand here. I'll be in the den." Then to Chrissy, "C'mon, sweetheart."

Chrissy trotted after her and leapt onto the couch.

Autumn dialed Stephanie.

"It's the bride-to-be! How are you holding up?"

"Pretty well, considering. I have so much help from exceedingly competent people who care about me, it makes it easier to prepare for Ray to move in. And prepare myself for all the changes coming in a matter of days."

"I can only imagine."

"Speaking of changes, Judge Cromwell can't marry us because her son is being questioned regarding the Curry murder."

"Do you think he did it?"

"Maybe, maybe not. Ray is trying to find out what he knows. But the judge doesn't want anyone to think Ray is playing favorites if she has a personal relationship with us."

"That's understandable," said Stephanie, crossing Terri Cromwell's name off the bachelorette party list. "Who did you get instead?"

"Mayor Snyder."

"That's cool. He seems like a nice guy."

"Yes, and he already RSVP'd that he's coming to the wedding with his wife. Makes it easier."

"Adam is excited about the dog and bachelor party."

"So is Ray. It's the perfect solution. He doesn't like to stay up late or be in a crowded public place."

"Your house is the perfect setup. All to make sure Chrissy doesn't miss you."

"How about me missing her? We've never been apart. It's strange to think about."

Chrissy rolled over to get a belly rub, and Autumn accommodated her.

"The spa was adamant about their no-pet policy. Not everyone finds it relaxing to be around dogs."

The moans and groans from the Shih Tzu made Autumn smile. How could someone not relax when playing with a pup? Research shows they can reduce blood pressure, stress, anxiety, and depression. And they encourage exercise and playfulness. For Autumn, Chrissy saved her and changed her life.

"We'll have fun. Bea wants to make sure we're all going in the sauna."

"If Bea commanded it, I will make it so."

They were laughing when they hung up.

Ward brought in a package addressed to Autumn, delivered by a private courier service. She opened it cautiously. Everyone watched.

"A clock!" Autumn said. "It's lovely."

She searched the box, but there was no card.

"A clock as a wedding gift is a bad omen in Chinese culture," said Bea.

"Signifying what?" asked Elizabeth.

"That someone is waiting for you to die."

Autumn dropped the clock back in the box as though it burned her. Perhaps Bea's interpretation was accurate.

"Should I put it with the knives in the shed?"

"I say get rid of both," said Bea, adamant that they were messages wishing Autumn harm.

Autumn nodded her agreement.

Ward took the box and put it outside in the freezing cold. A blast of frigid air swept through the reception area and made the women shiver.

Autumn picked up Chrissy and hugged her close.

"Who is doing this?" Elizabeth wanted to know.

"I don't know, but it's gone way beyond weird to downright disturbing," said Autumn.

"Maybe someone you forgot to invite to the wedding?" asked Elizabeth.

"I can't imagine who."

"Well, enough is enough!" said Bea. "Someone means business, and not in a good way."

"How about Faith Halifax?" asked Ward, returning to the group. "She was fit to be tied last time she was here."

"And Ray paid her a visit since then," said Autumn.

"Just to be safe, stay away from town. If you need something, one of us will get it," said Bea.

Kim Stokes came in and heard Bea.

"I'm in, but what are we talking about?"

Elizabeth said, "Autumn just got another package with a more serious message than the other one."

"What was it?"

"A clock."

"Sounds like a nice gift."

"Unless you know that it's a death wish for the recipient in Chinese culture," said Bea. "So it's all hands on deck to keep Autumn safe."

"We're still having the bachelorette party, aren't we?" asked Kim. "We'll all be together and away from here."

"I don't see why not," said Elizabeth.

"I vote we cancel," said Bea, her tone urgent.

"Maybe we should," Autumn agreed.

"I'll call Ray," said Ward. "He needs to know about this."

Ward walked into the study and dialed Ray. He explained what happened.

"The delivery van was navy blue, unmarked, with a Pennsylvania license plate first three digits were AWR. Sorry, I didn't get the rest."

"It's a start. What did the driver look like?"

"Medium height, male, short dark brown hair under his cap. No logo on the hat or anywhere on his jacket."

"Sounds like a private individual trying to make money for the holidays," said Ray.

"Anyone could have hired him."

"And he probably doesn't keep records. Might be an all-cash side business. Still, if we find him, he could have information to identify the customer."

"I'll keep an eye out here."

"Thanks, Ward."

Autumn's phone rang. It was Ray.

"I'm sending Adam to your house until I get there this evening. We don't know if whoever is sending these packages knows where you live, since they keep coming to the mansion."

"Okay," said Autumn, drained and nervous.

To the group, she said, "Ray wants me to go home."

"I'm going with you," said Bea, putting on her hat, scarf, coat, and gloves.

Autumn knew she couldn't say anything to talk her out of it, so she allowed her to get in the car with them.

"Let's talk about something other than wedding curses and murder," said Autumn.

"Suits me, as long as we can turn up the heat."

Autumn knew Bea preferred to roast than to freeze. She turned up the heat on the floor. To blast heat out of the upper vents made her face feel like it was cracking.

"Who are you bringing to the wedding?"

"Jasper. Ever since the Halloween party, things between us have progressed."

"How far has it gone?" Autumn grinned and wiggled her eyebrows.

"Get your mind out of the gutter. He's such a nice guy and treats me better than anyone ever has."

"I'm happy to hear that. Especially after that last one. He was truly nuts." Autumn reached over and squeezed Bea's hand. "No more of those!"

"Jasper is such a gentleman. He takes care of everything at the house and makes me feel cared for at the same time."

"You certainly deserve it. Sounds like he's a keeper."

"He's so excited about the wedding. He bought an expensive suit for the occasion!"

"Let's make sure he gets to wear it more than once. I'm hoping to have charity events and formal gatherings at the mansion."

"When people see the space for the wedding and how Elizabeth transformed it, it'll be an easy sell."

They pulled up to Autumn's house. Adam's squad car sat out front. She hit the garage door opener and pulled in. Adam came to meet them.

"Never a dull moment, eh, Autumn?"

She rolled her eyes. "Come on in. I'll make hot chocolate."

"I'll never say no to that!"

Beatrice was already in the house building a fire in the den when Autumn came in holding Chrissy. She wiggled to get down and ran to the sliding door. Autumn let her out. She tread slowly on the patio, ran up the steps, squatted, and then took a running leap into the snow, sinking up to her shoulders in the newest layer. She stuck her face in a drift, then hopped out and worked her way toward the door.

Autumn waited with the towel. Chrissy shook off before coming inside. Autumn took off Chrissy's coat, wrapped her in the towel, and kissed her damp face.

"Was that fun?"

Chrissy's tail went wild.

"Sit with Aunt Bea while I make some hot chocolate."

Autumn went into the kitchen and got a warm cloth, then handed it to Bea.

Bea worked on the clumps of snow stuck to Chrissy's legs, face, and ears.

"You silly girl," Bea said.

In the kitchen, Adam sat at the table, watching Autumn.

"You can make yourself comfortable in the den, Adam. I'll be in soon."

"Ray instructed me to stay with you."

She had no energy to argue.

❄ ❄ ❄

Pamela Brown brought the latest news to her listeners courtesy of the unknown delivery guy who'd gone to the Peabody Mansion earlier that day. In a previous broadcast, she'd asked listeners to update her directly with any news of the wedding or the murder. Pamela had an anonymous hotline where individuals left tips on a recording.

People loved sharing gossip as much as they loved hearing it. There were several calls with rumors about Barry Cromwell being arrested for murdering Angela Curry. Another that his mother, Judge Terri Cromwell withdrew from the wedding and that the wedding may not take place because they couldn't find anyone to marry them. And, finally, that Harry and Faith Halifax had conspired to kill Dr. Curry. But the best one was that someone was sending anonymous gifts to Autumn as a warning. What were they warning her about? Was there something about Ray that Autumn had to watch out for?

The podcaster couldn't verify any of it, but that didn't stop her from sharing these tips with her audience. And they ate it up.

❄ ❄ ❄

Steve and Mickey stopped by with news. While Chrissy and Mickey bounced a ball and ran back and forth in the den, Steve told everyone about the news on Pamela Brown's podcast.

"You don't have anyone to perform the ceremony?" asked Steve.

"Yes, we do. Why would she say that?" asked Autumn.

"She promotes the rumor mill," he said. "That's her entire show."

"Maybe this is a good thing. People thinking the wedding is off might take the focus off of you," said Adam.

"Hard to say, since we don't know who's doing it or why," Autumn said.

"Are you still having the ice sculpture?" asked Steve.

Mickey and Chrissy galloped past, batting a stuffed squirrel squeaky toy across the floor.

"No. We don't know if they're involved in Dr. Curry's murder, but we can't take the chance."

"Another thing gone wrong with the wedding!" said Beatrice. "If we had it on Wednesday, none of this would have happened!"

"Maybe you're right, Bea, but Elizabeth had another idea that's even better," said Autumn.

"What's that?"

"She found a wood carver to create the tree with our initials on it. That way, we can keep it forever."

"I like that idea," said Steve. "After all, you're paying for it. Might as well have a keepsake that lasts. Ice just melts."

"Exactly," said Autumn.

Bea shook her head.

"Let's hope nothing else happens, that's all I have to say."

"You made things turn out fine. I'll trust the candied almonds and bells to save the day," Autumn said, patting Beatrice affectionately on the back.

❄ ❄ ❄

Ray and Ace went into the front entrance of the hospital. The receptionist asked them to wait while she called Dr. O'Brien to the desk. He showed up moments later.

"I'm so sorry to tell you this, but Barry left the hospital. We couldn't hold him."

"When did he leave?"

"We're not sure, but it was sometime this morning."

"No one called me!" said Ray, frustration in his voice.

"I'm so sorry, Lieutenant. It was during a shift change."

"Were you able to get any information out of him since I was here last?"

"Nothing."

"I have to go," said Ray, and gave the doctor a curt wave. "C'mon Ace!"

He dialed Adam as he pulled out of the hospital parking lot.

"Barry Cromwell left the hospital. We don't know when he left or where he went. Stay sharp!"

"Will do!"

"Another call is ringing through, let me take this."

Ray picked up the other line.

"Lieutenant Reed."

"This is the forensic lab calling about that ice sculpting tool you brought in. We found blood near the handle, and it's a match for Dr. Angela Curry."

"Thank you."

He dialed Chief Stanley.

"Dr. Curry's blood is on Halifax's tool."

"I'll send two officers to pick up Harry and Faith Halifax."

"Also, Barry left the hospital. We're looking for him now."

"Keep me posted."

❄ ❄ ❄

Autumn called Stephanie to share the latest developments.

"We're going tomorrow, no matter what," said Stephanie. "I understand that you're concerned about Barry Cromwell and Harry and Faith Halifax, but you'll be away from all that."

"What if Faith is the one sending me these terrible gifts? She's mad at me and has a short temper," said Autumn.

"They arrested her, didn't they?"

"Yes, but she could be out by tomorrow."

"Is this really about leaving Chrissy?"

"No. I don't want to be vulnerable."

"You'll be with eight women who no one in their right mind would want to mess with."

"True."

"See you in the morning."

⸙20⸙

Barry Cromwell's jacket alone wasn't enough to keep him warm. Without gloves, his hitchhiking thumb was numb. He pulled his hands deeper into his jacket sleeves and shoved his left hand deep into his fleece-lined pocket while keeping his right visible to oncoming motorists.

Most passed him by. Some hit melted snow puddles and soaked the pant leg facing the street. Barry's pace slowed as he navigated the knee-high snow piles along the side of the road. When he couldn't see cars from a couple miles down the road, he faced forward and stuck both hands in his pockets.

He'd never walked this stretch of road. His mother had always driven him back. He felt the sense of relief coming off her as they got closer to Tree Crest, his live-in facility. Barry didn't share that he felt the same, eager to get back to where the staff and other patients understood him and gave him medication that soothed the chaos in his mind.

The driver stowed heavy winter coats into the spotless trunk, and the women piled into the shiny black stretch limousine; their excited chatter sounding as though they all talked at once. Autumn was last, as she assured her fur baby.

Autumn hugged Chrissy and kissed her face.

"Mommy is going out, and you're staying with Daddy. I'll be home soon."

She handed her to Ray, reluctant to leave her and wishing she could come to the spa.

Chrissy tried escaping Ray's grasp, trying to follow her mommy and looking confused as to why Autumn would leave without her. She barked urgently, calling to Autumn. Guilt swept over her, sad to leave Chrissy behind. To Autumn, it sounded as though Chrissy was crying, *Mommy! Mommy!*

Maybe this wasn't such a good idea after all. But everyone was here and having fun already, so it was too late to call off the party. Maybe they could eat earlier and get home sooner.

Autumn looked back and waved. Ray did his best to calm Chrissy, even showing her Ace and Mickey, who stood on either side of him in the doorway.

Ray waved and called out, "Have a good time. Don't worry!"

But she did worry. Chrissy's trauma losing her original pet parent, Gary Martin, and sitting with his dead body overnight instilled a sense of abandonment that subsided only when she was with her mommy. It took every ounce of will she possessed to trust that Chrissy would calm down, surrounded by her daddy and furry friends.

Autumn got into the limo next to Stephanie, who put a hand on her arm.

"She'll be fine," said Stephanie.

"This is the first time we've been separated since I got her."

"I know."

The limousine took off, and the women took turns pouring the pre-mixed Mimosas. A basket decorated with tulle and ribbons held individually wrapped, pre-cut bagels, cream cheese, and jelly. Fruit was in another container and plenty of napkins to go around.

Laughter and chatter intensified as the drinks made the women lightheaded. At the halfway mark to the spa in the Poconos, Autumn's eyes became heavy. Despite her best effort to keep them open, she couldn't, and was soon deep asleep, with her head against Stephanie's shoulder.

❄ ❄ ❄

Barry saw the limo whiz by. He was halfway home and the white sedan coming down the road stopped. He hoped this last ride would take him the rest of the way.

The sun was out and the roads wet from the melting snow. He didn't have much to say to the driver until he saw the black limousine parked on the shoulder stuck in a snowdrift.

He asked the driver to slow down a bit and saw that the limo driver's window was down and the driver sat slumped over the wheel.

The driver of the sedan pulled in front of the limo and dialed 911. Barry asked him to wait and got out of the car. The limo driver didn't move as Barry approached the car.

Barry knocked on the back passenger door and heard moaning. He tried the handle, and it opened. A bunch of women were inside, slouched to the side and leaning against one another. One looked familiar. She batted her eyes and looked at him.

"Barry?" she said, groggily.

He couldn't remember her name, but remembered that he met her at his mother's house. She was with another woman and a little dog.

She held her head with her hand and pushed the women to either side of her, trying to wake them up. She looked around the limo.

"Where's Autumn? Did you see her? The woman who was with me at your mother's house?"

Barry looked around the car and came back, shaking his head no.

The driver of the sedan came up next to Barry. "I called 911. Is everyone okay?"

The women were in various stages of awakening, moaning and holding their heads while they got their bearings.

"I think someone drugged us, and our friend is missing."

"Same for your driver. He's out cold, so you're not going anywhere until the police get here."

"Barry, what are you doing here?" asked Stephanie.

"On my way home. He's giving me a ride," Barry pointed his thumb at the driver.

"Ray is looking for you."

Barry shrugged.

Stephanie held her head in her hands.

Beatrice moved and looked around her. "What's going on? Where's Autumn? Who's this?" she said, pointing to Barry.

"That's Barry Cromwell, the judge's son," said Stephanie.

Beatrice, not one to mince words, said, "You're the crazy one?"

The driver of the white sedan decided he'd had enough and left without saying a word.

"Thanks a lot!" Barry said, his anger growing. "That was my ride!"

"I'm sure the police will be happy to give you a ride back to New Hope," said Stephanie.

"I didn't do anything!"

"So you say." Stephanie rubbed her temples.

The other women were groaning.

"Who made those mimosas? Way too strong." Elizabeth said, sounding drunk.

"Someone drugged us," said Stephanie. "I don't know who made them. The container was already in the limo when we got in."

"Maybe if we eat something, the effects will wear off," said Kim Stokes, reaching for a bagel.

Some grabbed bottles of water and guzzled them down.

Barry turned to leave just as the police car pulled up next to the limousine. The officer arrested him and put him in the back of the cruiser.

With Barry secured, the officer peeked his head inside the limo. "Everyone okay in here?"

Stephanie explained and asked if an ambulance was on the way for the limo driver.

The officer checked the driver, determined he was still alive, and called for an ambulance.

"I can take us home once they pick up the driver."

"Is this your limousine?" asked the officer.

"Uh, no."

"Then you can't take this vehicle. The limo company has to send another driver."

"Ugh." Stephanie's displeasure echoed among the other women. Stephanie gave him the name of the limo company.

"Sorry, ladies."

The officer turned and spoke into his radio, asking for support regarding the missing bride-to-be and for dispatch to contact the limo company.

"I'll stay with you until they get here."

Stephanie pulled out her cell phone and dialed Ray. After telling him as much as she knew she hung up and took a swig of water.

"He's on his way and bringing the cavalry. Pups and all."

"Whoever took Autumn will be sorry," said Carol Reed, a growl under her breath.

"I guess the bachelor party is off," said Julie Hall, calling her husband Brad. She told the story and hung up. "He and Teddy are coming to get me. We can give anyone else a ride who wants one."

Stacy Eldridge, Kim Stokes, Lisa Coleman, and Elizabeth Johnson took her up on the offer.

"I'm staying here and getting the new driver to follow Ray. I want to be there when we find Autumn," said Carol Reed.

"Me, too," said Stephanie.

"Wait until I get my hands on whoever did this!" said Beatrice Peabody.

❊ ❊ ❊

"She's waking up."

"Be quiet!"

Autumn's head felt too heavy for her neck. How could one Mimosa knock her out and give her the hangover of a lifetime? She couldn't see, and her shoulders ached. When she went to touch her face, her hands couldn't move, tied behind her back. She flexed against the rope, but it wouldn't budge. She sank into the thickly cushioned chair on which she sat, making it difficult to stand up. The rope around her ankles didn't help either.

A hand gently stroked her hair. She moved her head away, disgusted at the touch of this unknown person. She tried to move to the side, but another hand shoved her back.

Autumn wondered who these people were. She couldn't ask with a gag around her mouth.

She heard a bang across from her, like feet stomping on a hardwood floor. A musty, earthy smell came across her nostrils.

Someone pulled down the gag enough that the rim of a glass touched her lips. No odor came from whatever was in it. She assumed it was water, but didn't trust her captors enough to take a sip. She turned her head, and they withdrew the glass and put the gag back into place before she could yell or ask questions.

Autumn felt a chill and realized she wasn't wearing her jacket. She heard someone stacking logs and balling up paper. A click of a lighter and then crackling. At least she'd get some warmth soon.

The banging against the floor again. Muffled cries for help. Another captive was in the room.

Autumn responded in kind, letting the other person know they weren't alone.

A robotic voice said, "Knock it off!"

Autumn assumed it was some type of app that changed your voice. She couldn't tell if it was male or female.

The captors monitored what was going on. Trying to get away right now wasn't an option. The woozy feeling still fogged Autumn's brain, so she opted to save her strength for now.

❊ ❊ ❊

The ambulance took away the drugged limo driver, still unconscious from whatever the kidnappers used on him, and the first officer to arrive on the scene escorted Barry to the New Hope Police station for questioning. Brad Hall loaded the women into his SUV. Teddy, the Yorkshire terrier, jumped up and down when he saw his mommy, as though it had been a year since they were last together.

A few minutes after everyone was on their way, Ray pulled up. With him was his dad, Steve Coleman, Ward Everly, Adam, Ace, Mickey, and Chrissy.

"Everyone okay?" Ray asked.

"Yes," said Stephanie.

"We're going with you to find Autumn," said Carol.

"You're staying here until the replacement limo driver gets here," Ray firmly answered.

"We're freezing," said Beatrice.

"The engine's running with the heat on," said Ward.

Beatrice glared at him and he caught the daggers she sent him without blinking.

"It's safer for you to stay here," Kevin Reed said.

"We need to stay with the limo anyway," said Stephanie, with a subtle elbow to Beatrice.

"I guess," said Beatrice.

"Fine. We called the limo company and the driver should be within the next twenty minutes," said Kevin Reed.

Ray added, "We'll call you as soon as we know anything."

The women watched as the band of men and canines went off to find their beloved Autumn.

❄ ❄ ❄

Autumn worked the knot that held her hands together, trying not to tip off her captors by moving her arms. She listened for clues as to who they might be, but their caution was in their favor. Autumn thought of Chrissy and Ray, hoping they could feel her. She didn't know where she was, but with her connection to the two beings she loved the most, she trusted they'd find her.

A large hand stroked her leg, and she jerked it aside to get away from the unwanted touch. Autumn resented being yanked from her thoughts of Ray and Chrissy. With the removal of the hand, she went back to creating an energetic connection with her loved ones.

116

Ray likely would use his investigative skills to find her and wouldn't pick up on thoughts she sent his way. But with Chrissy's telepathic ability when they were together, she wondered if she could signal her from a distance. It was worth a try. There was nothing to lose.

❄ ❄ ❄

Ray kept an eye out for any side roads that went into the woods. Where could the kidnappers have taken Autumn? In the Poconos, there were various communities, many gated, and even more separate cabins nestled into the woods.

"You know what just occurred to me," said Steve from the backseat.

"What?" Ray asked.

"Maureen Roberts told me and Autumn that Megan Harris has a cottage up here. She sold everything and moved up here."

Ray glanced in his mirror.

"That might have been helpful to know an hour ago!"

"Well, I just remembered."

Ray paused.

"Sorry, I'm just worried."

Kevin Reed patted his son's shoulder from the passenger seat.

"Anybody know Maureen's number? She would have the address," said Ward.

Steve did an internet search on his phone and found her office number. He hit the link and put it on speakerphone.

"Maureen Roberts. How can I help you find the perfect home?"

"Maureen, it's Steve Coleman. Autumn's been kidnapped. We're in the Poconos and thought about Megan's cottage. Do you have the address?"

"I'm not sure I can give you that."

"Maureen, it's Ray Reed," he shouted into the speaker. "Megan may be able to help us. Please give us the address."

There was a pause, nails clicking on a keyboard, and then she gave the address.

"Please let me know when you find her. If I hear anything, I'll call you back."

Ray and Steve thanked her simultaneously and hung up. According to the GPS, they were fifteen minutes away.

❄ ❄ ❄

Autumn's bladder needed the bathroom. She tried saying the word against the fabric of the gag. One kidnapper understood, grabbed her upper arm, and shoved her forward. She almost tripped, and could only hop with her ankles restrained. Using the voice app, the person warned her not to take off her mask or gag as they released her arms.

"I'm standing right here, so don't get any ideas."

Autumn rubbed her wrists and shook out her arms, trying to get blood flowing again. Not knowing if the person in the bathroom with her was male or female unnerved her. She made it quick, and they guided her, hopping back to the chair. They retied her hands, this time in front of her.

Settled back in the chair, her thoughts turned once again to Chrissy.

❄ ❄ ❄

Five minutes away from Megan's cabin, Chrissy started whining and pawing at Steve's leg.

"What's wrong, Chrissy?" he asked.

She looked at him and whined louder than let out several barks, similar to when Autumn got into the limo without her.

"Don't worry. We'll find your mommy," Steve assured her.

Steve couldn't appease Chrissy, and she wiggled, barked, and whined. As they got closer, she became inconsolable and tried climbing into the front seat. Steve held onto her little body as best he could.

"We're almost there," said Ray.

"Maybe Chrissy senses her mommy," said Steve.

"If anyone can, it's her," Ray said, without revealing Chrissy's secret.

Down a dirt road, the cabin came into view. It was a cozy log cabin with lace curtains on the windows. Two cars were outside, a black sedan and an olive-green Jeep, neither one recognizable to Ray or anyone else in the car. He parked sideways, blocking the driveway.

"I'll be right back," Ray said, closing the door to keep the heat in.

Chrissy was going crazy, and Steve finally let her leap into the front seat. She stood on her hind legs and scratched at the window, almost as though digging her way out.

Ward got out and stood next to the truck, ready to back Ray. He held a bat in his right hand, just in case. Adam got out, too, hand on his sidearm.

Ray knocked on the door. He waited and then knocked again.

"Megan, it's Ray Reed. We need your help!"

He heard shuffling inside. He turned to Ward and Adam, pointing around the back. They spread out to cover both sides of the house. He tried the door, but it was locked.

"Megan, you okay in there?" Ray shouted.

He went back to the SUV and let Ace out of the car. Ace bristled and waited.

"Anyone else in there?" Ray yelled.

"Gotcha!" yelled Adam, wrestling a person in a parka to the ground.

Ace came running and stuck his face inside the parka's hood, teeth bared and snarling. The kicking stopped. Ray stood over them.

Kevin Reed opened his door and Chrissy jumped out of the vehicle and dropped a distance to the ground. Mickey pushed past to follow.

The person in the parka kicked and screamed. "Let me go!"

Ward snuck around the back, looking for an opening. Chrissy came charging past him, followed by Mickey.

"Chrissy, no! Mickey, get back here!" called Steve, chasing after them.

Kevin Reed got out of the vehicle to cover the front door.

Steve saw Chrissy run inside the cabin, Mickey in hot pursuit, and followed.

Steve took in the scene all at once. Autumn tied in a chair. Another woman tied up across from her, and a large man standing in the middle of the room.

Chrissy ran at him, and he kicked her to the side. Chrissy squealed and fell over. Mickey saw him do it and went after his leg, barking and growling. Steve had never seen Mickey so upset, but figured he was protecting his friend.

"Ray, in here!" Steve yelled.

Ward came through the door, ready for battle. He swung the bat and connected to the man's midsection.

Mickey's sharp teeth punctured holes in the man's jeans, blood soaking through.

Ace entered the scene and launched himself at the man's chest, knocking him over and pinning him to the ground, saliva dripping from his massive incisors.

Steve untied Autumn and removed her gag and blindfold.

"Baby!" she held her arms out to Chrissy, who limped over to her mommy. Autumn scooped her up and held her close, careful of any injuries. "Oh, my baby!" She covered her head in kisses. "Are you okay?"

Ray came in the back door with Adam, holding the other kidnapper by the scruff of the jacket.

Ward untied the other captive.

"Megan! Oh, no!" said Autumn.

"Autumn, it's all my fault," she sobbed. "I'm the one that gave them information about your gown and other things. I'm so sorry." She put her face in her hands, crying.

"No wonder you never got back to me," Ray said to William Moore. He didn't call Ace off of him. Served him right.

Another vehicle pulled into the driveway, gravel crunching under the tires. Car doors slammed and the sound of running feet. Someone banged at the front door.

"Let us in!"

Steve opened the door. Carol Reed, Stephanie Douglas, and Beatrice Peabody stormed in, ready for a fight.

"What are you doing here? I told you to wait by with the limo," said Ray, exasperated.

"Our driver arrived a minute after you pulled away. We followed you," said Carol.

"How did I miss that?" Ray said, rolling his eyes toward the ceiling.

"I'm a private detective for my other job. Surveillance and following cheating husbands undetected are my specialty," said Frank Pangborn, handing Ray his card.

"That figures," said Kevin, chuckling.

"Who do we have here?" asked Carol, pointing at the person struggling with Adam.

Adam pulled the hood down.

"Brittany Farmer? But why?" Autumn asked, stunned.

Ray looked more closely at Brittany and squinted his eyes. Staring, he tilted his head to the side and pulled off her scarf. He lifted her hair and pulled her ear forward, revealing a tattoo that read *Ray* in tiny clean script. She had gotten it right before they had broken up to prove her love for him. It served to make him realize then more than ever that her possessiveness was something he couldn't live with. She wasn't the right woman for him.

He stepped back.

"Patty?"

She looked at him, an evil grin on her face.

"It's not too late to marry me instead, lover."

"Not likely," Ray said.

"Patty Myers?" Carol said, shocked. "You don't look the same."

"Plastic surgery. It was a riot talking to you, Carol. You had no idea it was me." Her laugh had no mirth.

Carol sauntered over to her son's ex-girlfriend, looked her in the eye and said, "Well, if I ever want to know where you are from here on out, all I have to do is visit you in State prison."

"Nothing like committing a felony to get free room and board for the next 20 years," said Beatrice.

Ace growled and licked his lips.

"Okay, Ace, good boy!"

He barked one last time in William's face, spraying him with spittle, and moved off his chest.

Adam handcuffed Patty Myers. Ray handcuffed William Moore. Ward stood close by, bat at the ready in case either of them tried to escape.

Stephanie had her arms around Autumn and Chrissy.

"Which one of you nut bags drugged us?"

"Detective Moore here makes a mean mimosa, doesn't he?" Patty said, throwing him under the bus.

William Moore glowered at her. "Just you wait."

Autumn wiggled out from Stephanie's protective grasp, but held onto Chrissy.

"I still don't get it," said Autumn. "What did I ever do to you?"

"Ray is mine, not yours. I tried scaring you off with the gifts, sabotaging your wedding invitations. Anything to get you to cancel the wedding. But you're like Suzy Cream Cheese, always finding the positive in everything."

Beatrice pointed an accusing finger. "You cursed the wedding! How dare you!"

"The good news is, your plan didn't work, and Autumn is marrying Ray," said Stephanie.

"William, why would you do this to us? Ray was your friend. And you kicked Chrissy!"

"People do crazy things for love. I wanted to be with you. Once I located Brittany, and she explained her plan to disrupt the wedding, I was in. If the wedding got canceled, you could be with me."

Autumn had a disgusted looked on her face. "You touched me when you had me tied up! How could you think I'd leave Ray for you or anyone else?"

William Moore shrugged. "I love you."

"That doesn't give you the right to make the choice for both of us. I love Ray!" exclaimed Autumn.

Megan got bowls of water for the dogs. Ace and Mickey lapped up every ounce and went for more. Defending their people was hard work.

Chrissy, snuggled deep in her mommy's arms, and didn't want any.

"I want to get Chrissy to a vet. She was limping."

"Yeah, let's wrap this up. Adam, Ace, and I are taking these two for processing."

"There's plenty of room in the limo for everyone else!" said Carol.

"I'll call the spa and tell them we're not coming," Stephanie said.

"We'll meet back at our house tomorrow evening and have a combined bachelor and bachelorette party," said Autumn.

"That works. I'll call everyone and let them know." Stephanie had it handled.

"Autumn, I'm so sorry for everything," Megan said, hardly able to look Autumn in the eye.

"I wish you a peaceful life, Megan."

Autumn walked away, eager to get Chrissy checked out.

The first stop was to an emergency vet clinic close to Megan's cabin that Stephanie found on the GPS. X-rays showed no broken bones, and other diagnostic tests showed no internal injuries. The exam revealed bruised ribs and a sprained leg. The veterinarian gave Autumn a bottle of an anti-inflammatory drug, some liquid pain killer in a syringe to take orally, and prescribed cold compresses. In the meantime, she gave Chrissy a shot of anti-inflammatory and a mild pain medication.

"Don't let her jump on or off furniture for at least a week," the veterinarian told Autumn.

"We can do that," Autumn said, relieved.

Back in the limousine, Beatrice poured scotch from a fresh bottle they got at a nearby liquor store while Chrissy got examined. Now that the crisis was over, scotch was a nice way to relax all the way home. The limo dropped everyone off at their own homes, so no one had to drive.

Autumn got in the door, carried Chrissy to her spot outside, and then got her fur baby settled. She fed her from a little bowl so she didn't have to stand on her sprained leg. Snuggled in their favorite chair, Autumn gently applied the ice pack for ten minutes.

"Let's go to bed, sweetheart."

Autumn carried her outside one last time and then into the bedroom, where they both fell asleep within minutes.

⇕**21**⇕

Ray and Adam got back to the New Hope police station and locked up the kidnappers in the local jail cells under Ace's watchful eye. Next stop, Ray went to see Chief Stanley, while Adam filed a formal report.

Ray told him what happened while a medic took care of Moore's dog bite injury and broken ribs.

"What do you mean William Moore kidnapped Autumn and held Megan Harris captive?" the Chief blustered.

"He wanted to stop the wedding and Patty Myers, a.k.a. Brittany Farmer suggested Megan's cabin as the perfect place to wait out the wedding date."

"I'll go talk to him. In the meantime, Barry Cromwell is in the interview room waiting for you. We'll bring out Harry and Faith Halifax individually when you're ready. Nice piece of work retrieving the murder weapon."

"Thanks, Chief."

Before talking to Barry, Ray wanted to speak with Barry's mother, Judge Terri Cromwell, about what she might remember from that night.

"Hello, Judge, this is Ray Reed."

"Hi, Ray. Was Mayor Snyder available to perform the ceremony?"

"Yes, everything is fine. I appreciate you maintaining integrity in this case."

"Of course."

"The reason I'm calling is I'm about to question Barry."

"I can't believe he made it as far as he did before they found him."

"He was fairly close to his treatment center. As for now, we need to determine what, if anything, he had to do with Dr. Curry's death. What do you remember about that night?"

"I thought Barry was in his room, but when I went to check on him, he wasn't there."

"Do you know where he went?"

"I don't. Sometimes when he's home, he goes for walks at night. I remember he returned around ten o'clock that night."

"Thanks, Judge."

"You're welcome, Ray. I know you'll follow the clues until you solve this murder case. Wherever it may lead, I support it."

"Much appreciated."

Ray and Ace went down the hall and heard Barry yelling that he wanted to go back home to the Poconos. Ace's ears turned to home in on the sound. Ray went to the cooler and poured Barry a cup of water.

"Ace, you need to stay out here, okay?"

Ace stood a post next to the door.

"Good boy!"

Ray entered the room.

"Hey, Barry. You must be thirsty." Ray put down the paper cup.

Barry grabbed it and guzzled it down.

"Let me out of here!"

"We'd really appreciate your help in finding out who murdered Dr. Curry. Can you do that?"

"Dr. Curry! She's gone!"

"Yes, and if you can remember anything from the night she died, we might catch the killer."

"I don't know anything!"

"Are you willing to try something? For Dr. Curry?"

Barry paused at her name and finally nodded.

"Think back to the night before Dr. Curry was found dead."

Barry frowned.

"What were you doing that night?"

"Out walking."

"It was cold. Where did you walk?"

"Main Street. Near Dr. Curry's office."

"Did you see anyone outside of her office?"

Barry shook his head.

"What did you see?"

"White van. Said Halifax on the side."

"What else can you remember about the van?"

"It was open."

"What do you mean by open?"

"The back door. It wasn't shut all the way."

"What did you do when you saw the door open?"

"I looked around, and then I looked inside. It was dark, so I clicked the door shut."

"At this point, were you the only one on the street?"

"Yes."

"Then what happened?"

"I saw a man run out of Dr. Curry's office, so I hid in the shadows."

"What can you tell me about him?"

"He looked upset. He didn't see me. He ran over to the van, got in, and drove away."

"Did he use a key to get into the vehicle?"

"Yes."

Barry licked his lips.

"You're doing great. Want some more water?"

Barry nodded. Ray got it for him. Barry took a pill from a container in his pocket and washed it down with the water.

"Can I see that?"

Barry handed over the pill bottle. The label had his name on it, with instructions to take it once a day with food. Ray handed it back.

"Do you eat granola bars or chips?"

"Doesn't matter."

Ray went to the vending machine and got him both. He slid it across the table. Barry munched on the chips first.

"Ready?"

Barry nodded.

"After the van pulled away, what did you see?"

"Someone standing in the alley next to Dr. Curry's office."

"Male or female? Tall or short?"

"I'm not sure. They were in the shadows. I saw them move, but couldn't see who it was."

"Did they see you?"

"I don't know. I'm good at hiding. Especially in the dark."

"Did you hear them say anything?"

"No, it was quiet."

"Were they alone?"

"I guess. I didn't see anyone else."

"Then what happened?"

"I cut through the alley behind me and walked around town for a while. Then I went home."

Barry peeled the wrapper off the granola bar and took a bite.

"Did you see Dr. Curry at any time that night?"

"No. I would have talked to her."

Barry took another bite of the granola bar.

"Is there anything else you can tell me about that night?"

Barry chewed.

"There was a lady walking around a couple of blocks over."

"What can you tell me about her?"

"She was wearing a quilted jacket, scarf, a hat with a ball on top, and jeans and walking fast."

"A ball on top?"

"Yeah, made of yarn."

"A pompom?"

"Yeah."

"Did you see her face?"

"No. She was looking down."

"Did you see anything else?"

"One car went by another block over. A dark color."

"Did you see the driver?"

"No. I was half a block away."

Barry crumpled the wrapper and stuck it in his pocket.

"Thanks, Barry. I appreciate your help. Call me if you think of anything else."

Ray handed him his card. Barry took it and shoved it in his back pocket without looking.

"Your cell phone is at the front desk if you want to call for a ride."

"Since you guys brought me here, you should bring me home. Back to the mountains."

"Can't do that, but I'll bet your mom will come get you."

"Yeah, sure."

Ray walked Barry to the officer at reception and got his phone back. Barry strolled out of the police station. Ray observed him to be in a world of his own. Barry's mental illness and medications may have put him in a state where he believed the version of the story he gave Ray. Either way, there was no concrete evidence.

Ray hadn't learned much from the interview with Barry. He wondered if Barry had lied about that night, although his story was plausible.

Ray's fatigue from the long, crazy day made him postpone his interviews with Harry and Faith Halifax. Their arrest for possession of an instrument of crime gave him leeway to schedule them first thing in the morning. It would also give him time to think about his approach and consider what they'd already told him—how much was true and what they were lying about. It was better to talk to them with a clear head.

Brain fog set in as he came down from the fear of potentially losing Autumn. It was getting late, and he just wanted to be with her.

He loaded Ace into the SUV and pulled away from the police station, thinking about Patty Myers and how, after all this time, she kept track of him and set out to stop his wedding. Chiding himself for not being aware of her presence so close to home, he gripped the steering wheel, angry he had put Autumn in danger. How did he not see the extent of her psychopathology when ending the relationship? He believed her controlling nature was too smothering for him to commit to a long term relationship. He did not know the extent to which she'd go to keep him in her life. His underestimating her could have cost Autumn her life. William Moore may have been the only thing standing between Patty and Autumn to keep her safe.

Although safe was a relative word. He had an inkling that Moore had feelings for Autumn, but missed how consuming his desire for her was. Both Ray and Autumn were victims of obsessive love, and it frightened him. Twice, his instincts failed him, putting Autumn in the path of danger. Did his job and his past put her at risk? Was it fair to marry her and expose her to criminals who might resent him and seek to harm him or his family? As her husband, he needed to do better.

For now, those who threatened her were behind bars. But it wasn't good enough. He couldn't be there all the time. Autumn had friends, neighbors, and loyal staff who looked out for her. He wanted to find out how she felt about what happened and the level of protection she wanted. He didn't want to be overbearing, but didn't want her to suffer another PTSD episode over recent events.

Ray pulled into the driveway of what would soon be his residence. He turned off the engine and looked at the dark house and went through a mental checklist of improvements: motion sensors, lights on timers, alarm system, cameras. He glanced at Ace in the rearview mirror.

"How about spending more time with Autumn and Chrissy, buddy?"

Ace let out one loud bark.

❄ ❄ ❄

Ray used his key to open the front door, stepped inside, and locked the bolt behind him. The house was quiet. He flicked on the light switch and placed his keys in the bowl in the entryway before wiping Ace's feet using the black and green towel Autumn designated for him. It hung beside Chrissy's white and peach striped one.

Ray and Ace padded down the hallway to the main bedroom, turning on the light as they went. The door was open and two shadow forms occupied the bed. Torn between letting them sleep and checking on them, he opted for the latter and sat gently on the bed.

"Ray?" Autumn said, groggy from her deep sleep.

"Yes. Go back to sleep. Just wanted to check on you."

"No, I'll be up all night if I do that."

Chrissy stirred next to Autumn.

"You okay, sweetheart?" Autumn shifted lightly to avoid jostling Chrissy. "Ray, turn on the small lamp, please."

Dim light from a sixty-watt bulb filled the room.

Chrissy lay next to her mommy, bleary-eyed.

"She probably has to go out." Autumn got up slowly. She lifted Chrissy from the bed, careful to keep her comfortable, and headed for the back door.

Ray knew the drill and got their coats to bundle them up before heading outside in the freezing cold. He let Ace out and stood with Autumn and Chrissy, watching as Autumn helped her precious Shih Tzu stand and go potty without putting weight on her sprained leg.

The care with which Autumn treated Chrissy extended to Ray and Ace, and he looked forward to a lifetime with her, but still had to ask her an important question.

They got settled back inside. Autumn fed Chrissy and Ace, propping Chrissy on a pillow so she could sit while eating. She opened cans of soup for herself and Ray and pulled out thick seeded bread for dunking.

They took their meal into the den, and Ray made a fire. Autumn turned on the Christmas tree lights and left the rest off. Chrissy lay beside Autumn on the couch. Ace lay on the floor at Ray's feet. The dim light soothed their nerves. Comfortable silence surrounded them as they ate.

Ray put his empty soup mug and bread plate on the cocktail table and cleared his throat.

"How are you feeling?" he asked Autumn.

"Tired, but okay, all things considered."

"Think it might be a good idea to see Dr. Harper? He helped you through PTSD from the car accident. Being kidnapped could cause a resurgence of symptoms."

Her mouth tightened and eyes squinted the way he'd seen many times when considering something important.

"Maybe. I can at least call him and see what he thinks."

"Good." Ray rubbed her leg.

"What else? Something's on your mind."

Ray hesitated and then came out with it.

"I'm responsible for putting you at risk."

"How do you figure that?"

"My crazy ex. Someone I worked with obsessed with you. I missed both signs, and you suffered because of it."

Autumn held his hand.

"You also came to get me."

"It never should have happened in the first place."

"So, you're not allowed to be human?"

"Not when it comes to you. I'm supposed to keep you safe, but I don't know if it's possible with the job I have."

"What are you saying?"

"There are many times when I can't be with you and dealing with criminals who might try to harm you to get to me..."

"Neither of the people involved in this were criminals we know of, anyway. There's no way you could have anticipated what they'd do. I'd say the epicenter of the craziness revolves around Angela Curry. Both of them were her patients."

He pressed his lips together.

"I'm afraid that me marrying you compromises your safety."

She paused.

"Are you saying you don't want to get married?"

"I do, more than anything. I can't imagine life without you and Chrissy. I want to make sure you've thought this through."

Autumn smiled. Her eyes softened. She squeezed his hand.

"I think about marrying you more than anything else. It's the right decision. Deep down, in my bones, it feels right."

Ray was quiet.

"Hey," Autumn said, and he looked at her. "Don't think you're getting out of this. We're getting married day after tomorrow. We have our party tonight, and the best wedding ever to look forward to. Besides, life would be boring without our adventures."

"Then I have a security plan that includes technology around the house, lighting, and Ace spending more time with you two."

Ace's head popped up at the sound of his name.

"That's right, buddy,"

Ace looked at Autumn and Chrissy and put his head back down.

"He'll certainly make sure no one gets to us. The way he took down William Moore was right out of a movie."

Autumn laughed. The sound lifted Ray's heart.

"And do you really think your mother is going to sit idly by? I wouldn't want to mess with her."

It was Ray's turn to laugh.

"She's a powerhouse, that's for sure."

"What about Beatrice?"

"A force to be reckoned with!" admitted Ray.

"Let's see. Ward Everly is another one who has surprising skills."

"That he does."

"I'm surrounded by formidable people. You don't have to do this alone."

"True," Ray said, hope in his voice.

"Best of all, I'll have you and Ace to sleep with every night. I'm the most protected woman on the planet!"

"You're right. I'll be here every night."

"I'll sleep soundly knowing you're next to me."

He kissed her, feeling more love than he thought possible, silently vowing to hold her close and keep her safe.

Ray stayed over that night but barely slept. He thought about Autumn's point that the person at the center of the chaos was Dr. Angela Curry. Dr. Curry may have thought she was in charge, but everything fatally blew back on her in the form of a stab wound to the chest.

❄ ❄ ❄

While Ray was managing his situation at home, Chief Stanley sat across from soon-to-be-former detective William Moore and glared at him. Moore, shackled to the interview table, looked tired and small.

"Last chance to tell me what you were thinking, Bill."

William Moore shook his head.

"You know the charges you're facing for kidnapping one woman, holding another hostage, in her own home, no less, and conspiring with a fugitive."

Moore shrugged.

"I'll only talk to Ray."

"Fine, spend the night in a cell, and we'll talk more tomorrow."

Autumn woke to Chrissy watching her. Ray wasn't in the bed. The clock read eight thirty. He likely left over an hour ago. Ace sat next to the bed, head above the top of the mattress, panting.

"Okay, let's go outside!"

She pulled on her robe, shoulders aching from being tied up, her back stiff from fear and being shoved around. Chrissy let Autumn lift her from the pile of blankets and carry her outside. Ace charged outside the moment the sliding door opened wide enough for him to escape. Autumn didn't put Chrissy through manipulating her to get her coat on. She held her securely while she went and wrapped her in a warm blanket once they were back in the house.

A tapping on the front door sent Ace barking. Chrissy didn't react. Maybe the pain killer dulled her response. Autumn looked out the peephole to see who it was. Ray promised to install a camera so she could see who it was on a screen before opening the door. It was one of the many security strategies he planned for after the wedding. This time it was Steve and Mickey, so she opened the door.

Mickey pranced in and sniffed Chrissy through the blanket Autumn held her in. He and Ace acknowledged each other.

Steve stomped his feet on the welcome mat outside the door and came in behind Mickey. He held two to-go cups in his hands.

"Looks like you could use this," he said.

"Thanks. Please bring it in here so I can put her down."

They went into the den, and Autumn made Chrissy comfortable on the couch before taking the steaming hot cup from Steve.

"Hazelnut roast," she said, smelling the blend. "Heavenly."

"Did I wake you?"

"No, we were up, but not for long. Can you watch Chrissy for a minute while I change?"

It took two minutes to throw on sweatpants and a cable-knit sweater. Back in the den, she reclaimed her cup and took a sip.

"So good."

"How are you feeling? I see the little one is on bedrest."

"You saw what she went through. I can forgive a lot of things, but not someone kicking my baby."

"How long does it take to heal?"

"Depends on keeping her off the leg, which we're doing. The doctor said if we're diligent, it could be six weeks."

"She won't be able to walk down the aisle at the wedding."

"Elizabeth ordered her a pink wagon for her to ride in. That was the plan anyway, to keep her feet warm, but it turned out to be a good idea all around."

Autumn petted Mickey, who came over to check on his little friend.

"You're a hero, Mickey!"

He wagged his tail.

Ace came over and looked at Autumn, as if to say "what about me?"

"You, too, Ace!"

He gave one loud bark.

"Now what?"

"Ray is questioning everyone today down at the New Hope police station. He wants to wrap this up before the wedding."

"Doesn't give him much time. It's tomorrow. Nothing like putting a little pressure on yourself."

"Sometimes he sets goals a little too high. As long as Brittany, er, Patty and William Moore are behind bars, I'm fine with it."

"How about the murder investigation?"

"He's talking to Faith and Harry Halifax today. We'll see what happens."

Steve nodded.

"Lisa wants to come over early and help Stephanie set up for the party tonight."

"Works for me. I'm in a daze after yesterday."

"You sure you're up to it?"

"Having everyone here makes me feel safe, so, absolutely."

In that moment, she realized the trauma of the day before had affected her. She needed support beyond family and friends. After Steve left, she called Dr. Harper's office and made an appointment for after the wedding.

❄ ❄ ❄

Ray checked in with Chief Stanley before scheduling the suspects for interviews. He learned that William Moore had provided no useful information the day before and hoped his new questioning strategy would crack the wall he put up.

He spoke with Harry Halifax first.

The man looked broken and exhausted. He looked at Ray, his formerly steady gaze blank.

"I didn't sleep at all last night. I don't think I'll be much use to you."

"Tell me about the murder weapon."

"It's a tool I use for ice carving."

"How did you use it the night Angela Curry died?"

"I didn't. It was in my truck."

"After you left Dr. Curry's office, did you return with the tool?"

"No, I never went back in. Haven't we been through this before?"

"Let's go through it one more time. You may remember something you didn't mention before."

Ray's experience questioning suspects told him the story sometimes changes, especially when fatigue sets in.

"I left her office and got into my van."

"Did you see anyone on the street?"

Harry thought for a moment and rubbed his forehead.

"I'm not sure. I just wanted to get out of there."

"Did you hear anything?"

Harry's eyes lit up.

"The back door of the van clicking shut."

"When did you hear the sound?"

"As I ran toward the van, but I didn't see anyone."

That was consistent with what Barry told him. Barry hid when he saw Harry running toward the vehicle. Whoever was in Harry's van before Barry got there likely took the tool.

"Where did you go after you pulled away?"

"Home. I wanted to be there in case Angela called."

"Was your wife at home?"

Harry looked at the ceiling.

"No, but she came in a short while later."

"Where was she?"

"She said she ran to the store."

"What items did she buy?"

"Come to think of it, she didn't have a bag or anything. I don't know. I didn't ask, because I was too worried about what Angela planned to do."

"Thanks, Harry. That was helpful. I'm going to release you."

"What about Faith?"

"I need to speak with her, but you can go home. Get some sleep."

Ray had a strong sense that Harry was a philanderer, but not a murderer. His wife, on the other hand, was still a suspect. Barry recalled seeing a woman on the street a couple of blocks over.

By the time Ray got a cup of coffee, officers had settled Faith at the table. Her furrowed brow and down-turned mouth conveyed her anger. If she could have shot flames from her eyes and burned Ray to a crisp, she would have.

"How dare you keep me in that stinking cell overnight!"

Ray ignored her commentary on the state of the jail. He knew the place was spotless, and that she meant the display of self-righteousness to set-up the power dynamic between them. He took his time setting up his notepad and coffee, catching Faith looking at the steaming cup while he did so.

"Want a cup of coffee?"

To say yes would hand power back to Ray. She hesitated before nodding.

"How do you take it?"

"Cream, two sugars."

Ray called the officer from the hallway and asked him to get the drink. He stayed silent until the coffee came and the door closed. She took a sip and closed her eyes. He sensed relief. Maybe a little caffeine would help improve her mood.

"Tell me about the night Dr. Curry was murdered."

"I was home. I told you that before."

"We have an eyewitness who says he saw you walking a couple of blocks away from Dr. Curry's office that night."

Faith took another sip of coffee.

"I ran to the store to get milk."

"Last time we talked, you said you were home when Harry arrived. Now he said you came in after he did."

"His memory is horrible. I don't expect him to think clearly. He's an artist."

The creative people Ray had met over the years were some of the clearest thinkers he'd known. That reasoning didn't fly for him.

"When you walked to the store, did you see anyone?"

"One guy walked past me on the sidewalk."

"Did you recognize him?"

"No."

"Anyone else?

"Detective Moore drove past in a dark-colored sedan."

"How do you know it was Detective Moore?"

"I didn't know until later. He'd been in the shop the day after. That's what made me remember him."

"What did he want?"

"He asked about ice sculpting and what tools we used. He said he was thinking about taking it up as a hobby."

Ray made a note.

"Were you anywhere near Dr. Curry's office that night?"

She hesitated and clenched her fist. Ray waited.

"I was in the alley when she came out of her office."

"What were you doing there?"

"Trying to catch my husband in the act, but his van was already gone."

"When did you see Detective Moore drive by?"

"Not until after I walked a couple of blocks over. That's when he drove by."

"Do you remember hearing anything after you saw Dr. Curry?"

"As I walked away, I heard someone grunt and then a thud, but I thought nothing of it."

"Why not?"

"A couple of minutes after, the snowplow went by. I figured that's what made the noise."

"What did you do after hearing the noise?"

"Kept walking."

"And when did you see Detective Moore?"

"I saw his car when I got two blocks over."

"How did he seem?"

"It was dark. I glimpsed him when he drove under the streetlamp. There was a woman in the car with him."

"Did you recognize her?"

"No."

"Anything you can tell me about his expression or his mood?"

She finished the coffee and tapped the empty cup against the table.

"No. Like I said, it was dark."

"When did you empty your husband's van?"

"The afternoon after the murder."

"Was everything in its proper place?"

"Harry isn't the most organized person. The tools were scattered on a tarp."

"How about the one with blood on it?"

"In a pile with the rest. Usually, Harry puts it back in his holster. But, like I said, he doesn't always put things back where they belong."

"When was Detective Moore at the studio?"

"That morning."

He thanked Faith and signed her out of the station.

The interview produced more information than he'd hoped for. Now to find out what William Moore was doing in the vicinity of Dr. Curry's office. He was waiting for Ray in the other interview room.

Ray brought a paper cup of water with him and gave it to William Moore, who scowled at Ray and the cup.

"Hi, Bill," said Ray.

"Isn't questioning me a conflict of interest?"

Chief Stanley walked into the room and sat down.

"Not with the Chief sitting here. Besides, you're on record as requesting me specifically."

Chief Stanley crossed his arms and pinned Moore with a steady gaze.

"It doesn't change the fact that Autumn will be mine soon enough."

Ray squinted at Moore, deciding whether he was deep in delusion or just taunting him.

"At what point did you and Patty conspire to kidnap Autumn?" asked Ray, refusing to be goaded.

"Didn't know you and Patty were an item until I found who I thought was Brittany Farmer. She told me how disgusted she was that you and Autumn were getting married."

"What was her plan and how did you get sucked into it?" asked Chief Stanley.

"I figured if she wanted Ray and could stop the wedding, I had a better chance with Autumn."

He looked at Ray and said, "She liked it when I touched her at the cabin."

Ray didn't take the bait.

"What were you doing in the vicinity of Dr. Curry's office the night of her murder?" asked Ray.

"I wasn't."

"We have a witness who says you were."

"Angela Curry lived on the main drag in town. A lot of people were probably in the area that night."

"Not according to several people who were present," said Ray, watching for a change of expression.

Moore shrugged.

Chief Stanley jumped in. "Bill, you and Ms. Myers are up on kidnapping charges."

William Moore had no reaction.

"Patty had everything figured out."

"Megan is pressing charges against both of you. You held her hostage."

"Patty knew about the cabin. Nothing personal."

"Tying up two women against their will is a big deal," Chief Stanley said. "You know this."

"Love is the most important thing. That's what Dr. Curry didn't get."

"What do you mean?" asked Ray.

"Patty told me that Dr. Curry tried talking her out of interfering with the wedding. Said it was time she found a new love."

"Did Patty Myers have anything to do with the death of Dr. Curry?"

William Moore thought about it.

A knock on the door interrupted them. Adam came in.

"Ray, can I see you for a minute?"

Ray went with Adam into the hallway.

"I've been talking to Patty Myers. She has a lot to say about how William Moore coerced her into the kidnapping scheme."

"Interesting, since he's saying it was her idea. Go back and tell her she's getting the blame and see what she says."

"On my way."

Ray called Chief Stanley into the hallway, updated him, and then went back into the interview room.

"My lawyer said I don't have to answer your questions," said William Moore. "So did my union rep."

"We can get them both here within the hour if you'd like. Until then, we'll postpone this interview, and you can wait to find out what Patty Myers is saying about you," said Ray.

William seemed startled. Ray thought his behavior was odd, given his history with the police force. He knew procedure and his rights. He could have asked for his lawyer right after his arrest, but he hadn't. He also refused a phone call.

The Chief chimed in. "Bill, we're just trying to understand what happened. If you need a therapist or anything else. You're one of us."

Moore seemed to relax at the Chief's words.

"No, that's okay. Let's talk. What lies is Patty telling about me?"

"She said you're the mastermind behind the kidnapping plan."

"Patty told me Autumn would think it a romantic gesture to take her and profess my love for her."

"It didn't turn out that way, now did it?" said Chief Stanley.

"Instead of a therapist, you may need a dating coach instead," said Ray with a smirk.

William Moore tried reaching across the table to grab Ray, but the pain of broken ribs and handcuffs restricted him.

Stephanie, Autumn, Carol, Beatrice, and Lisa gathered at Autumn's house to set up for the party. Having them there was soothing for Autumn, despite the commotion they created. She even got to take a quick nap with Chrissy while they continued working. It was short enough that the nightmares of being held captive didn't creep in like they had the night before. Thank goodness Ray was there to wake her when she began moaning and pulled her from William Moore's clutches, as he had the day before.

Ace stood watch over everyone, including Chrissy. If she tried getting out of her bed, he nudged her back in.

The clinking of glassware and plates, the heavenly smells of pie, cake, and cookies baking, and the loving support they provided bolstered Autumn. The sound of the technician installing the new security system Ray ordered helped, too. Ward Everly watched his every move, making sure there was no funny stuff going on, like the ability to hijack the system.

Ray had hired off-duty police for the wedding, and everyone was on alert, making sure no one else crawled out from under a rock to spoil their special day. Autumn prayed that Patty Myers and William Moore would stay in jail until long after the ceremony.

Adam faced Patty Myers at the interview table. He couldn't imagine Ray being with someone like her, so defiant, angry, and self-absorbed.

"What do you want from me?" she asked him.

"The truth. How did the plan come about? Whose idea was it?"

"Megan invited us to her cabin." Mischief twinkled in her eyes.

"Megan made a different statement. Did you know William Moore before this incident took place?"

"I'm not telling you anything unless I get a deal. This was all Bill's idea."

"I'll make sure to tell the D.A. that you cooperated."

"No dice. I want my lawyer."

Adam terminated the interview until Patty's lawyer arrived. Once he did, they conferred, and the interview continued.

"I met him at Dr. Curry's office. She tried to talk me out of pursuing Ray. Made me mad. Bill was in the waiting room. He saw how angry I was."

"And then what happened?"

"He contacted me after his therapy session to tell me Dr. Curry told him the same thing about Autumn. Threatened him with revealing his love for Autumn."

"So, what did you do?"

"After my attempts at scaring Autumn into calling off the wedding, he called my cell and said he had to meet me on police business. We met outside of town and talked about a plan to stop the wedding."

"What did the plan include?"

"Getting rid of Autumn so I could have Ray. Bill said he'd take her. It was all his idea."

"What did he need you for?"

"To arrange going to the cabin and trick Megan into letting me go there."

"How did Autumn end up there?"

"Bill knows the owner of the limo service and told him he was on security detail for Autumn. They let him check the limo, and he put a large container of mimosas with crushed up tranquilizers in it."

A ruckus down the hall halted the conversation.

"I have information pertinent to the case! I'm telling you, I know who killed Angela Curry!"

Then the chief's voice boomed. "What's going on out here?"

Adam got up from the table and went to see who was out there.

"Don't you know who I am? I get the scoop on everything in this town, and this is big!"

It was Pamela Brown. Adam thought he recognized the voice from her podcast.

"I saw his car that night!"

"Whose car?"

"William Moore's car."

"Where did you see it?" Ray had joined the party out front.

"Near the Halifax studio."

"When?"

"The morning after the murder."

Ray took her back to a vacant office. Adam and Chief Stanley joined them.

"Now, Ms. Brown, what did you see?"

"William Moore threw something in the back of Harry Halifax's van."

"Did you see what it was?" asked Ray.

"Didn't get a hard look at it, but he took it out of his coat pocket. It was in plastic. He pulled it out and threw it back there."

"Where were you located?"

"I was in the bushes across from the studio."

"Why were you in the bushes?" asked Adam.

"I needed a scoop for my podcast. William Moore stopped feeding me information, so I followed him."

"Why didn't you come forward sooner?" asked Chief Stanley.

"Because I wasn't sure it meant anything. But then I heard you picked up Harry and Faith Halifax for possession of the murder weapon. Then you let them go. It dawned on me that William Moore may have placed it in the van."

Ray wondered what happened to the plastic bag. Maybe it was in Moore's apartment.

"Thank you, Ms. Brown. Are you willing to sign a statement to this effect?" Ray was ready to nail down this testimonial so they could get a search warrant for Moore's place.

"Yes, as long as I can have the scoop on your wedding this weekend."

"Sure, why not," said Ray. It was a small price to pay to nail a murderer.

They found the plastic bag with Angela Curry's blood on it in a jacket he kept in the hall closet. They had Patty Myers's confession regarding conspiracy. They corroborated Patty's story with the limousine company owner. William Moore was up for murder, drugging a car-full of women, kidnapping, and holding someone hostage.

Patty tried one more time to hit on Ray.

"Now is it my turn? I gave you what you needed."

"Don't flatter yourself. You never gave me what I needed, which was freedom."

He didn't mention the love and freedom Autumn gave him. Leaving her name out of it was best. If Patty got out of prison sooner than expected, no telling what she'd do. Her delusion was strong, and she might attempt to harm Autumn.

Ray concluded a full day and was ready to party like it was the night before his wedding. But he had to break the news that Pamela Brown would attend the wedding. He wasn't sure how that would go over.

≈ 23 ≈

It filled Autumn with joy to see the den, kitchen, and dining room filled with friends and neighbors chatting away, eating, and drinking. She could see Chrissy snuggled in her cozy bed away from the foot traffic, but close enough for her to keep an eye out if Chrissy needed anything. Ace was in a bed beside her. Steve brought another dog bed and placed it in the circle for Mickey to join. It was like a canine healing circle with Ace and Mickey caring for their friend.

Ray walked over to Autumn. The thought of marrying him tomorrow was everything she dreamed of. But the serious look on his face made her pause.

"Everything okay?"

"Sure, sure. I just need to tell you something," he said.

"Should I sit down? Guzzle this wine? You're making me nervous."

He smiled. "It's about a deal I made."

She waited, bracing herself.

"Pamela Brown came to the station with a key piece of information that helped us nail William Moore for the murder of Angela Curry."

"Okay, and..."

"She's coming to the wedding tomorrow to cover the event for her podcast."

"We agreed to avoid the press for this event."

"I'm sorry, but isn't it more important to put a killer behind bars?"

"Absolutely, especially that one. To think I was under his control. Thank goodness you found me!"

"With Pamela's information, he's going away for life instead of just 20 years for kidnapping you."

"In that case, an extra guest isn't such a high price to pay."

She hugged him. "People will talk about the event no matter what, so what the heck. Maybe she'll speak highly of those responsible for the magical atmosphere and get them some exposure."

The crowd started thinning, leaving behind lots of empty wine and beer bottles strewn on counters and tables. Crumbs left behind on serving platters, coffee cups, and mostly empty coffee pots awaited attention.

"Time for you to go, Ray! Don't want to jinx things just before the wedding. We've made it this far," said Beatrice.

"I wanted to stay to make sure Autumn is okay," he said in mild protest.

"I'm staying upstairs," she said.

"So am I," said Stephanie.

"Besides, we have to clean up," said Lisa Coleman, who lived a few houses down the block.

"You guys have done enough," said Autumn.

"Not quite. After tomorrow, we can call it a day. Right now, we're in it for the long haul," said Stephanie.

"Mom, Dad, go on home. It's going to be a long, wonderful day tomorrow. I want you rested," said Autumn to Carol and Kevin. It was the first time it felt natural to call them that.

Ray reviewed the new alarm system with Autumn and made her promise to arm it once Lisa left. She promised and pushed him out the door.

She went over to Chrissy for the tenth time that evening to check on her. She looked so alone without Ace and Mickey hovering over her. Autumn took her outside and put her in bed for the night before making sure the upstairs bedrooms were ready for Bea and Stephanie.

"You're such a good girl. I know this isn't as fun for you as we were hoping, but let's make the best of it and make sure you get well as soon as possible."

She kissed Chrissy's head and surrounded her with pillows and blankets to keep her leg secure.

"Mommy loves you."

She left the room with the small table lamp on.

Bea and Stephanie were chatting with Lisa when Autumn came back into the kitchen. They had so much energy.

"We can clean this up after the wedding," said Autumn.

"No way! We're not leaving this mess. Besides, we want a clean kitchen to make breakfast in the morning," said Bea.

"What are we having?" Autumn thought that the guests ate every morsel of food in the house.

"Eggs Benedict, my specialty," said Stephanie.

"It is? In all the years I've known you, I've never seen you make that." Autumn folded her arms.

"It's second only to my hot pot mac and cheese from college." Autumn and Stephanie had been roommates at Villanova.

"I admit, that was pretty good," Autumn said, smiling.

"Okay, then. Things look squared away here." Stephanie patted Lisa on the back. "You outdid yourself tonight."

"No, tomorrow is the day. Wait until you see the cake!"

"Oops, almost forgot," said Autumn. She went to the cabinet where she kept the antique cake topper Carol Reed gave her and presented it to Lisa. "This goes on top."

"It's lovely!" said Stephanie.

"Carol gave it to me. It's my something borrowed from their wedding cake."

"Thank heavens for that," said Beatrice. "I thought we didn't have the full complement of old, new, borrowed, and blue!"

"Sounds like the wedding is safe from all curses, Bea!" Stephanie teased her.

"Laugh if you will, but this wedding is completely safe from curses!" Bea declared.

"Especially since two crazy people are in jail for messing with Autumn," said Lisa.

"I can't imagine how scared you were," said Stephanie.

"It wasn't something I'd want to do again, that's for sure," said Autumn, a shiver going down her spine. "I just hope he's convicted and stays in jail for a long time. Same goes for Patty."

"I guess you can't tell what people are thinking or how far they're willing to go to get what they want," said Lisa.

"Bea and Lisa, you were both victims of some craziness yourselves. You know how traumatizing it can be." Autumn wrung her hands.

"True. Time healed us. It'll heal you, too," said Bea.

"Time and Dr. Harper. I'm calling him on Monday."

"Isn't he coming to the wedding?" asked Lisa.

"Yes, but I want him to have a good time, not talk about my problems."

"And you need to have a good time, too!" said Bea.

"Let's go to bed, so we're fresh in the morning," Autumn suggested.

"Right, the bride needs her beauty sleep!" said Stephanie.

Lisa left, they set the security alarm, and went to bed.

❊ ❊ ❊

The urgent blaring of the burglar alarm and the phone ringing woke everyone in the house at 2 am. Autumn shot awake and picked up the phone.

"This is the alarm company. What is your password?"

Autumn couldn't remember, so she said "I don't know."

"We are dispatching the police immediately," said the operator.

"I don't know what set it off!" Autumn yelled over the blasting siren.

Chrissy shook next to her. She put a thick blanket over Chrissy's head to try dulling the sound. Footsteps stampeded down the staircase and she saw a shadowy figure in her bedroom doorway. Autumn squinted to see who it was and then reached over for the light switch.

Brightness blinded her and then shed light on who was in her room. The siren pierced her ears.

"You'll never make your wedding! I'll make sure of that. Ray wants me. We're meant to be together!"
Patty Myers yelled over the sirens.

Autumn put her arms out in front of her as Patty charged toward the bed.

Autumn screamed. Patty tripped over Chrissy's extra-long squeaky toy laying on the floor and tumbled to the ground. Beatrice and Stephanie came running, brandishing heavy iron candlesticks from the dining room table and took turns hitting Patty's legs and torso, while screaming with the fury of banshees warning of death.

Autumn ran to the alarm panel and turned off the alarm just as the police banged on the door. She opened it and pointed to the bedroom, where they found Patty Myers defending herself from Beatrice and Stephanie. They moved the ladies out of the way and yanked Patty by the arm, then handcuffed her.

"This isn't over," said Patty, glowering at Autumn.

"Oh, yes, it is," said the Knollwood police officer. Autumn recognized him, but didn't know his name.

"Thanks for getting here so quickly!" Autumn said.

"We hope you and Ray have a great wedding!" said the other officer.

They hauled Patty out to the police car. Stephanie closed the door behind them.

Autumn ran to Chrissy, now shivering and salivating after the loud noise and the screaming. She held her close.

"My poor angel!"

Autumn wrapped her up in a blanket and brought her into the den.

"Wow, never a dull moment around here!" said Beatrice.

"Thank goodness we stayed over," said Stephanie.

"I'm ready to go another round," said Beatrice, holding the candlestick like a baseball bat. "She thinks it isn't over? Well, good luck with that. Next time we won't be so gentle."

A knock on the door. Stephanie stared into the video screen to see who it was. The neighbors heard the alarm. In marched Steve and Lisa Coleman with Mickey and Julie and Brad Hall with Teddy.

"Everybody okay?" Steve asked.

"Yes and no," said Stephanie, pointing to Autumn, trying to calm Chrissy.

Mickey walked over to his friend and licked her face, then made himself comfortable on the couch next to her. His presence seemed to help.

Brad made a fire and then walked the perimeter of the house to see how Patty had got in. A crowbar lay on the ground outside the flimsy laundry room door, the timber frame splintered. He closed it as best he could and used a shim to keep the door shut.

Julie made chamomile tea.

"The laundry room door needs replacing, Autumn," said Brad. "I recommend a steel door."

"Thanks, Brad," said Autumn.

They all sat in quiet support of Autumn and Chrissy, figuring there had been enough noise for one night. It was an hour before Chrissy stopped shaking and was willing to go outside to relieve herself.

They stood to leave around 3:30 am.

"Thanks so much for coming over, you guys," said Autumn.

Each hugged her in turn.

"We're always here for you," said Steve.

"We'll see you later today at the ceremony," said Julie.

"That alarm really worked," said Beatrice. "Maybe I should get one."

"Me, too. But how did Patty get out of jail?" asked Stephanie.

"Bail? I'm surprised Ray wasn't informed."

On cue, in walked Ray and Ace. They rushed over to Autumn and Chrissy, Ray hugging them tight.

"I'm sorry. No one called to let me know she got out on bail. I stopped at the station to make sure she's secured and unable to get out for any reason."

"Not your fault."

"The good news is we have William Moore locked up and facing trial for murder and kidnapping."

"Murder?" Stephanie asked.

"He killed Angela Curry for fear she'd spread the word about his feelings for Autumn."

"How stupid can you be?" Beatrice commented. "He goes through all that and then kidnaps Autumn. Everyone knows anyway."

"When did he do it?" asked Autumn.

"Harry left his van unlocked the night of the murder, so it was easy to steal the ice sculpting tool from the back. He waited until Harry left and no one was on the street in a shadowy area near her office. He watched until Dr. Curry came out of her office and crossed the street closer to where he stood. Then Moore attacked her and shoved her into a snowdrift."

"Did he dig it out and cover her back up?" asked Stephanie.

"He was lucky to have the snow plow go by minutes after he pushed her. She was dead, so he took off, and the snow plow did the rest."

Autumn's eyes filled with tears.

"All because of me," she said.

"This is not your fault," said Beatrice. "People do crazy things in the name of love."

"She's right," said Stephanie. "You did nothing to make him commit murder."

Ray put his arms around her. "Desperation and loneliness are to blame. It pushed him over the edge."

"Are we sure he's not getting out like Patty did?" Autumn asked.

"Yes. He can't afford the bail and the judge doesn't take kindly to law enforcement personnel committing heinous crimes," Ray assured her.

Her weak nod showed him how wiped out she was.

Stephanie took Chrissy and let her out before bed, holding her the way Autumn did to take the pressure off of her leg.

"We're staying here tonight," he said, staring at Beatrice.

Bea nodded.

They finally all settled in for much needed sleep before the big day.

A fresh dusting of snow from the night before made the property look as clean as a new beginning. The sunlight shining on the snow made it shimmer. The weather was crisp, with no wind to add to the chill of the day.

Ward cleared the parking area, paths, and ceremony area. He lit the gas heaters an hour before guests would arrive in the wooded wonderland under the sycamore tree.

Its trunk was white and complemented the snowy ground and white tulle Elizabeth strung along the bridal path. She wove pink and purple roses and baby's breath into the fabric for a pop of color that matched Autumn's bouquet. The men in the wedding party had a single purple rose boutonniere. The purple roses symbolized enchantment and splendor, while the pink represented femininity, grace, and true love.

Guests drove to the grand entrance of the Peabody Mansion and handed their keys to a valet who took the cars to the main parking lot next door at the Peabody Mansion. At the entryway, catering staff welcomed them with a flute of ice-cold champagne with pear, apple, and blood orange nectar in it. Serving the drink to the guests replaced having it come through the eliminated ice sculpture. Canine guests received a chewy snack. Staff hung coats and pointed them to the preliminary offerings set-up around a magnificent carved tree with Autumn and Ray's initials inside a heart on the trunk.

Armed security stood with board-straight posture in various locations throughout the reception area. Dressed in black suits, they looked like secret agents.

Friends, local politicians, business owners, and Peabody Foundation board members looked as elegant as the space as they mingled and munched in the reception area.

Meanwhile, the bride and her ladies readied themselves for the main event in the largest suite upstairs. They could hear murmurs from the increasing number of friends and business associates entering the grand space. They heard an occasional "ooh" or "ah" when a group walked through the door in admiration of the wintery theme created by Elizabeth.

"I'm exhausted," said Autumn, as the makeup artist did her best to cover the bags under her eyes.

"It was a long night, no doubt about that," said Stephanie. "But you look beautiful. Despite everything, your eyes are sparkling."

"I'm thinking about spending my life with Ray. He makes me so happy."

Carol beamed at her. "And you make him happier than I've ever seen, dear."

The makeup artist finished and stood back to admire her work.

"You're stunning!" said Stephanie.

Autumn smiled. "Thanks. And so is my little bundle of love over there," she said, pointing to Chrissy.

Chrissy had tiny pink silk roses and tulle adorning her collar. She looked regal on a faux fur blanket ready for the little wagon. Stephanie took over caring for the little princess so Autumn could get ready. They planned a group effort for the entire event to make sure Chrissy got what she needed in her compromised state.

The makeup artist worked on Stephanie, Beatrice, and Carol. The results were spectacular, and the women admired one another with joy and excitement.

A knock on the door and Kim Stokes walked in.

"All of you look amazing!"

"Is Ray here yet?" Autumn asked.

"Yep. Okay to lead the guests to the ceremony area?"

"We're ready," said Carol.

"It will take about twenty minutes to get their coats on and to lead them to the seating area."

"Okay," Autumn felt excitement well up in her chest.

"You're all lit up," said Beatrice. "I'm so happy for you."

"Thanks."

Kim came back when they were ready for the bridal party.

Ward helped the women down the steps, handed them their bouquets, and had Chrissy's wagon ready. He placed another faux fur blanket across her back, leaving the decorative collar exposed. Stephanie took the handle of the wagon and pulled it behind her. Kevin extended his elbow to Autumn, and she took it, looking at him and missing her father, but happy to start a new chapter. His hand was warm on hers, as he held her to him, steady and loving.

The sound of the string quartet playing Pachelbel's Canon in D floated through the air, adding to the magic of the moment.

Beatrice and Carol linked arms and walked first, pacing to the music, followed by Stephanie pulling Chrissy in the wagon. Guests made "*aww*" sounds at the sweet little fur baby riding by.

Carol and Beatrice took their seats in the front row. Stephanie and Chrissy stood to the left across from Adam, Ray, and Ace, who wore a black bow tie.

The gas heaters gave just enough warmth to make everyone comfortable in the clearing.

The guests stood as the bride entered. Many held their hands to their hearts at how beautiful she looked. Elbow-length gloves beaded to match the gown sparkled, as did her headpiece; a true winter bride.

Ray looked like a model in a tuxedo ad, his smile radiant when he saw Autumn. Autumn beamed at her groom. She glowed with joy and love.

Kevin delivered Autumn to his son, kissing her cheek and then sitting next to Carol.

The Honorable Josh Snyder stood out in his black suit against the white of the sycamore tree, having shed most of its bark and the surrounding snow-covered woods. He waved his hands, instructing guests to sit. A rustle of fabric, and everyone settled in.

The mayor began.

"It's been a long road getting to this special day, and we're thankful," he said.

Chuckling from the audience came from those who knew the details of what the couple had been through of late and the mayor's understatement of the circumstances.

"The couple thanks those close to them for their support in making this possible. I am truly honored to preside over this wedding for a couple so perfectly suited to each other. Their mutual love, respect, and understanding is a beautiful thing to see. The way they care for their friends, family, and community, and the way they honor their four-legged friends, brings great joy to those who know them. As you are here for each other and for those you love, so too we are here for you in challenging times and in times of gladness."

"The couple have written vows they'd like to share. Autumn, please go first."

"Ray, I love you with all my heart. And now blessings shine down on me as I get to spend my life with you. I adore your parents, too, and am grateful they have welcomed me with open arms into your family as Bea, Chrissy, and I welcome you. I promise to listen when you need an ear, to support when you need a friend, and to give unconditional love no matter the circumstances. With this ring, I give you my love, my devotion, and all the joy in my heart at sharing a life with you."

She slid the gold band onto his left ring finger.

Mayor Snyder said, "Ray, please speak your vows."

"Autumn, in my wildest dreams, I never expected to meet a woman so complete and loving. I'll be your rock, your protector, and your confidant. You can rely on me to stay true and to share the joys and challenges of pet parenthood."

The audience laughed softly.

"I'm grateful that I get to share my life and love with you and look forward to seeing what each new day brings. You are my one true love. Our adventures have only just begun."

He slid a diamond encrusted gold band onto her finger.

"By the power vested in me by the State of Pennsylvania, I now pronounce you married. You may kiss the bride."

Ray took her in his arms. Their kiss was deeper than in any romance movie. The guests stood, cheering and applauding and showering them with bird seed as the happy couple moved down the aisle, grinning ear to ear. The rest of the wedding party followed, practically skipping after them. Chrissy's wagging tail moved under the blanket and Ace pranced, his tail upright next to his daddy.

Back at the house, the party took off in high style. Piano music drifted through the air from a grand piano in the corner of the reception area. The string quartet and a flutist set up in the ballroom to play during dinner.

Although the gas heaters kept the ceremony area warm, the line at the hot chocolate station was long. Toppings ranged from the traditional marshmallows to whipped cream and mint stirrers. Peppermint schnapps and chocolate liqueur were also options for those not driving.

Autumn and Ray made the rounds. People patted them on the back and complimented the food and décor.

"You two sure know how to throw a party," said Dana Wood, friend, award-winning actress, and local resident.

"Dana! It's been too long." Autumn hugged her tight. "I know you have a tight schedule. We're so glad you could make it."

Dana hugged Ray.

"Congratulations! Wouldn't miss it. Elizabeth really outdid herself. If I ever get married again, I want to have the wedding here."

They all laughed, knowing what happened with her last husband.

"Or any other event you have in mind! At some point soon, let's just have a quiet evening together to catch up."

"I'd really like that," said Dana, hugging Autumn again.

In the corner, Pamela Brown talked into a digital recorder. Autumn walked over to her.

"Thanks for the information that put William Moore away."

"My pleasure," said Pamela, shutting off the recorder.

"I hope you don't plan to work the entire time you're here. Please enjoy yourself."

Autumn smiled at her and tapped one of the catering personnel.

"Pamela is a guest who didn't get a chance to place her dinner order. Can you please take care of that for me? I believe she's at Table 8."

Autumn looked at Pamela, who confirmed with a nod.

"Certainly!" he said, and walked over to Pamela to describe her options.

Julie Hall caught Autumn's attention before she heard Pamela's order.

"You look beautiful!"

"Thank you. So do you. Midnight blue looks great on you. Where's Teddy?"

"Over at the food and water station with Chrissy, Mickey, and Ace. Poor little Chrissy."

"That wagon came in handy. Who knew we'd need it for an injury?"

"She loves all the attention. People are stopping to pet her, and the catering staff are taking care of her every need, even feeding her by hand."

"So she gets to sit on her throne as she entertains her guests. That's how she rolls," Autumn said, laughing.

A Peabody board member was waving to Autumn. She hugged Julie. "Have a great time!"

She spotted Ray talking to Chief Stanley, who had his meaty hand on Ray's shoulder.

Chiming bells called the guests to their tables for dinner. Autumn and Ray sat with his parents, Beatrice, Jasper Wiggins, Stephanie, and Adam.

"Did you hear those bells ringing? Did you feel the positive energy?" Beatrice demanded.

"You were right," said Autumn, wanting Beatrice to feel good about her suggestions. "And the candied almonds are a nice touch, too."

She popped one in her mouth and crunched down.

"All that is well and good, but I must say you're a ravishing creature, Beatrice. Brains and beauty are an intoxicating combination." Jasper Wiggins reached out his hand, which she gladly took. He kissed her knuckles as he looked deep into her eyes.

Autumn wiggled her eyebrows at Ray, who smiled.

Someone started tapping on their glass, and then others joined in, signaling for Ray and Autumn to kiss, which they gladly did, followed by applause.

The love and joy surrounded the couple and all present at the event. When asked about their honeymoon, they excitedly said that they were moving Ray's things into the house. Some seemed disappointed by their choice, but the importance of this act was beyond the average person's understanding. This was what they'd been waiting for.

After dinner, they wheeled in the cake. Carol clapped her hands, seeing her cake topper. The couple cut the cake as cameras captured the moment. They fed one another daintily and kissed, smearing icing across their lips.

Sarah Kelly announced that the full dessert buffet was ready in the dining room, but asked guests to make a stop near the staircase so the bride could throw her bouquet.

Autumn climbed halfway up the winding staircase, turned her back to the crowd of single women below, and tossed the bouquet. She heard someone exclaim in joy. Turning to see who caught it, she saw Bea, happily clutching the bridal arrangement. Autumn noticed Jasper observing, an approving smile on his face. Autumn couldn't wait to throw Bea's wedding here. Everyone applauded and then headed for the glorious desserts that awaited.

The celebration lasted all week as friends and family helped Ray move from his apartment and get him settled at Autumn's house. She made it a point to say *our* house whenever she got the chance.

They served leftovers from the wedding and had plenty of wine to go around. Having their support team made the work fun and cut the moving time in half. In the process, Ray's parents got to know the neighbors and other friends better; a good thing since holidays and other gatherings included this group.

Two days after the wedding, Steve and Mickey came over with news.

"Pamela Brown featured your wedding and the murder investigation in her podcast. Of course, she gave herself ample kudos for helping to pin the murder on William Moore. She has it archived, if you want to listen."

They hit play.

"… and to all my listeners out there, the wedding of Autumn and Ray Reed was the most spectacular event I've ever seen. I expect the Peabody Mansion to become the wedding and event venue for miles around. The bride and groom were gracious hosts, welcoming me and making me feel comfortable. Who knew an heiress and her lieutenant husband were so down-to-earth?

"As for former detective William Moore, it couldn't happen to a nicer guy. He deserves everything he gets for killing Dr. Curry, even though she had an evil streak a mile wide."

"That's enough," said Autumn, stopping the playback. "He is mentally ill and needs help, not criticism."

"Pamela Brown's signature is exactly that. What amazes me is that she spoke so highly of the two of you."

"I'm sure we'll make her angry at some point," said Ray, ever the realist.

"Until then, let's count our blessings and be happy in this moment," said Autumn. "You never know how things can turn out for the best."

"Works for me," Ray said, and they clinked mugs of hot chocolate with peppermint Schnapps to seal the deal.

The End

Book Club Questions

1. Autumn and Ray chose not to live together before the wedding. Did you live with your spouse before your wedding? If so, do you think living together helped or hindered your relationship?

2. Ray and Autumn do not talk about their past romantic relationships. Do you talk about past romantic relationships, healthy or unhealthy, with your significant other?

3. Autumn is a very chill, go with the flow kind of bride. Were you like Autumn or were you a Bridezilla or somewhere in between?

4. Autumn and Chrissy have an extraordinary relationship. Have you ever felt a psychic bond with an animal who shared your life?

5. Did you suspect who the killer was? If so, what clues gave him/her away?

6. Bea puts a lot of stock in what some may see as superstitions. How superstitious are you? What, if any, are the "superstitions" you hold as true?

7. Who is the victim in the story? Is there more than one?

8. Autumn and Ray's wedding takes place in the winter. Would you want to get married in the winter or is there another season you'd prefer?

Recipes

Special thanks to Chef Jacqueline Peccina Kelly of StrEATS of Philly Food Tours for these fabulous recipes! All recipes by Chef Jacquie. Check out more at streatsofphillyfoodtours.com.

Pasta with Gorgonzola Cream Sauce

Ingredients:

- 8 ounces Gorgonzola cheese, roughly chopped
- 4 cups of heavy cream
- Pinch of freshly grated nutmeg
- 1/2 cup of walnuts
- Black pepper to taste
- 1 pound of cooked pasta (campanella, fusilli or farfalle shape
- 1 Tablespoon of fresh Italian flat leaf parsley, chopped, for garnish
- 1 Tablespoon of fresh grated Parmigiano-Reggiano cheese, for garnish
- 4 whole walnuts, for garnish. Toast nuts in a pan with butter for a few minutes, do not burn

Over high heat, in a large frying pan, bring cream to a boil then lower heat and simmer until reduced by half. Add a pinch of nutmeg and simmer for 30 minutes; stirring frequently until cream reduces to nappe, coats the back of a spoon.

When sauce is finished turn heat off and add cheese, stir until melted. Add nuts and stir and then add cooked pasta; toss until incorporated.

Place pasta on serving platter, garnish with chopped parsley, grated Parmigiano-Reggiano cheese and toasted walnuts.

Pasta with Radicchio and Pancetta Recipe

- 1 medium onion, sliced thin
- 2 Tablespoons of butter
- 2 Tablespoons of extra virgin olive oil
- 4 slices of pancetta or bacon, sliced
- 1 small head of radicchio, sliced thin
- 1/2 cup of dark balsamic vinegar
- 1 pound of cooked pasta (orecchiette or medium shells) and reserve some of the cooking water
- 1/2 cup of cherry tomatoes, cut in half
- 1/4 teaspoon of fine grade sea salt
- Fresh ground black pepper, to taste
- 1/2 cup of grated Parmigiano-Reggiano
- 1 Tablespoon of fresh Italian flat leaf parsley, finely chopped

In a medium saucepan over medium heat, add 2 tablespoons of butter and oil and onion, sauté until golden brown. Add pancetta, cook until crispy.

Add sliced radicchio and vinegar and cook until radicchio is wilted, taste and adjust seasoning with salt and pepper. Add tomatoes, pasta and a little pasta water and warm through, toss in Parmigiano-Reggiano cheese and serve immediately.

Garnish with chopped parsley.

Braised Short Ribs Recipe

- 6 beef short ribs (8-10 ounces, bone in)
- 6 Tablespoons extra virgin olive oil
- 1 large onion, diced
- 3 cups red wine (full bodied red wine)
- 2 cups beef broth
- 2 carrots, peeled and diced
- 2 stalks of celery, chopped
- 2 bay leaves
- 3 cloves garlic, coarsely chopped
- 2 Tablespoons of tomato paste
- 3 sprigs of fresh thyme

Preheat oven to 350 degrees.

In a deep and large braising pot, over medium/high heat, add oil and brown ribs on all sides. Remove ribs and sauté vegetables.

Add wine and bring to a boil. Add tomato paste, bay leaves, and broth then return ribs. Ribs must be completely immersed in liquid. Cover and transfer pot to oven and braise for 2 hours.

Chicken Saltimbocca al la Romana

- 4 Chicken cutlets about 5-6 ounces each
- 4 fresh whole sage leaves
- 4 Slices of Prosciutto di Parma
- 2 Tablespoons olive oil
- 2 cups white wine
- 2 cups chicken stock
- 4 Tablespoons of butter
- 1 teaspoon of kosher salt
- Fresh ground black pepper

Season chicken cutlets on both sides with salt and pepper. Place a slice of Prosciutto on top of chicken, a sage leaf and then secure with a toothpick for easier cooking.

Heat a large frying pan over medium-high heat, add oil and place chicken in pan sage side down and cook for 4 minutes. Turn chicken over and cook for another 3 minutes, until golden brown. Remove from pan and set aside, cover loosely with foil wrap.

Place pan back on the stove, add wine to deglaze, scraping all the bits from the bottom and sides of pan and reduce by half. Add stock and reduce by half.

Remove pan from heat and swirl in butter until sauce becomes thick and glossy. Add the chicken back to the pan to warm up and serve immediately.

Festive Salad with Champagne Vinaigrette Recipe

Champagne Vinaigrette Ingredients:

- 1/3 cup Champagne vinegar
- 1 teaspoon Dijon mustard
- ½ teaspoon honey or sugar
- 2/3 cup safflower oil
- Salt and pepper to taste

Prepare vinaigrette by placing all ingredients in a cruet or sealed container and shake vigorously. Vinaigrette can keep for a week if kept in sealed container in the refrigerator.

Salad Ingredients:

- 1 head of Bibb lettuce, rinsed, dried and torn to bite size pieces
- 2 Tablespoons of dried cranberries
- 2 Tablespoons of sliced almonds
- 2 Tablespoons of Smoked Gouda cheese, diced
- 4 Tablespoons of champagne vinaigrette

In a large bowl, add your salad, fruit, almonds, cheese and vinaigrette. Toss until leaves are completely coated.

Serve salad in a chilled salad plate or martini glass for a special festive touch!

About the Author

Diane Wing, M.A. is a multi-published author of dark fantasy fiction, cozy mysteries, and enlightening non-fiction. Her work helps people see the magickal, spiritual, loving side of life with a practical edge.

Diane is an avid reader, bibliophile, lover of trees and animals, and a lifelong learner. She and her husband are pet parents to a sweet little Shih Tzu named Sophie.

Connect with her and find out more at:

www.DianeWingAuthor.com

and www.DianeWing.com

The Adventures of Autumn and Chrissy Begin Here!

Only Chrissy, a cute little Shih Tzu, can unlock this mystery! Autumn Clarke survived the car crash that killed her parents. To help her cope with PTSD, she adopts Chrissy, a Shih Tzu with a remarkable secret. Chrissy is also the only witness to the mysterious death of her pet parent. Autumn vows to find the truth behind his death with the help of Chrissy, the neighbors and an attractive detective. Can Autumn unravel the clues while trying to heal Chrissy's trauma and overcome her own devastating emotional wounds in the midst of a dangerous murder investigation?

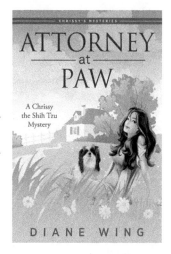

"Chrissy the Shih Tzu may be the cutest sleuth on the job, but don't let that button nose fool you—it's perfectly able to sniff out a killer with a little help from her human friends. Great start to a fun new series!"

—Sheila Webster Boneham, Author of the award-winning *Animals in Focus Mysteries*

"Diane Wing does an excellent job of showing readers just how animals can communicate with us through images and actions when we are tuned into their frequency. Through the relationship between Autumn and Chrissy, Wing also shows the importance of therapy animals and how much they can help those who need them. Add in a sweet romance to the intrigue of the mystery and you've got a book that you won't want to put down."

—Melissa Alvarez, Intuitive, animal communicator and author of *Animal Frequency* and Llewellyn's *Little Book of Spirit Animals*

"Diane Wing has created a wonderfully endearing little character in Chrissy the Shih Tzu. It really shines through that the author is an animal and dog lover. I can see these books quickly becoming a cherished addition to the cozy mystery genre."

—J. New, author of *The Yellow Cottage Vintage Mysteries*

Learn more at www.DianeWingAuthor.com

From Modern History Press

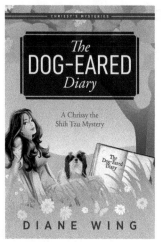

In this second installment in the series, Chrissy digs up clues to help Autumn solve a historical disappearance and a modern-day murder mystery

Autumn Clarke is getting her life back to normal with the help of her extraordinary shih tzu, Chrissy, when the death of a local philanthropist reveals the man's dark family secrets, as well as unexpected ties to Autumn. When Chrissy discovers a dog-eared diary in the dead man's family home, Autumn discovers that things in the Clarke family are not quite as they seem. Can Autumn interpret the hidden clues in the dog-eared diary to crack the most puzzling disappearance in Knollwood history? Are the recent murders connected to the past? Is Chrissy more insightful than Autumn realized?

"I have fallen in love with Chrissy and Autumn and their continuing journey to health while finding themselves in the middle of a murder mystery adventure. My pre-teen daughter and I enjoyed reading *The Dog-Eared Diary* and then discussing the clues, plot twists, and characters."

—Antoinette Brickhaus, Maryland

"Chrissy the Shih Tzu is a real character in the book and not just a prop to help the story along. Chrissy often felt like she was going to start talking. I loved the relationship between Autumn and her dog. The love the two of them have is absolutely perfect. Perfect for a rainy afternoon and one any cozy mystery fan will enjoy. I can't wait to see what happens next!"

—Andrea J. Guy

"I applaud the author for her use of so many clever writing devices within a rather brief cozy mystery. Nothing seemed contrived nor out-of-place. I hope that someone makes the decision to adapt these books to the screen because it would make one amazing mystery series!"

—Ruth A. Hill, journalist

Learn more at www.DianeWingAuthor.com

From Modern History Press

Prepare to be tricked & treated in this 3rd installment of the Chrissy the Shih Tzu cozy mysteries!

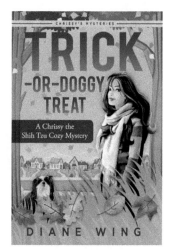

Fall has arrived in Knollwood, and Autumn Clarke is planning an elaborate Halloween event at The Peabody Mansion B&B to support the local animal shelter. With the entire town invited and the inn not officially open for overnight guests, an unexpected request lands Dana Wood, an A-list actor, as a long-term guest while shooting her latest movie in New Hope. Autumn and the gang step in to help with her baggage filled with betrayal, scandal, unsolved murder, a personal secret, and a cast of eccentric, suspicious characters. As the filming begins, Chrissy's shrewd judge of character and nose for unearthing incriminating evidence provide the backdrop for this twisty and thrilling tale.

Bonus features: book club questions, recipes of meals from the book, and a Halloween scavenger hunt list appear at the end of the book!

"Autumn and Chrissy have become my favorite crime solvers!! Diane Wing has put together another fun rainy afternoon, cuddle-with-my-dog in-a-corner-window mystery! Throughout this series we have seen Autumn and Chrissy overcome tragedy, find love, and solve some murders! All her supporting characters make sense and are loveable. A great read for anyone from 8 to 80!!"
—Antoinette B., Leonardtown, MD

"*Trick-or-Doggy-Treat* is a delightful, satisfying cozy mystery wrapped in the rich, colorful tapestry of a Pennsylvania fall in a wonderful town. Halloween has never been this enchanting. A truly enjoyable read!"
—Maxine Ashcraft, Oakland, CA

Learn more at www.DianeWingAuthor.com

From Modern HIstory Press www.ModernHistoryPress.com

CPSIA information can be obtained
at www.ICGtesting.com
Printed in the USA
LVHW080837140122
707701LV00002B/7